FADE

LISA MCMANN

SIMON AND SCHUSTER

First published in Great Britain in 2010 by
Simon & Schuster UK Ltd,
1st Floor, 222 Gray's Inn Road, London WC1X 8HB

A CBS COMPANY

Published in the USA in 2009 by Simon Pulse,
an imprint of Simon & Schuster Children's Division, New York.

Simon Pulse, and colophon are registered trademarks of
Simon and Schuster UK Ltd

A CIP catalogue record for this book
is available from the British Library

ISBN 978-1-84738-736-3

10 9 8 7 6 5 4 3 2 1

Printed by CPI Cox & Wyman, Reading, Berkshire RG1 8EX

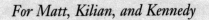

For Matt, Kilian, and Kennedy

ACKNOWLEDGMENTS

Many thanks to:

My fabulous agent, Michael Bourret.

My incredible editor, Jennifer Klonsky.

Sammy Yuen and Mike Rosamilia, who create the Best. Covers. Ever.

Matt Schwartz for way too many things to mention.

Lila Haber and Kate Smyth for their tireless promotional efforts and for always being available. Also to Victor Iannone and the awesome sales team; to Rick Richter, Paul Crichton, Bethany Buck, Lucille Rettino, Kelly Stocks, Bess Brasswell, Mary McAveney, Matt Pantoliano, Emilia Rhodes, Jeannie Ng, and Molly McLeod. Cassandra Clare, Chris Crutcher, Ally Carter, Richard Lewis, Lauren Baratz-Logsted, A. S. King, Melissa Walker, FanLib.com, and BookDivas.com.

All the awesome teen and adult reviewers and fans who plaster my books all over their websites and blogs.

My parents, siblings, in-laws, and outlaws for all the support.

Shout-outs to:

Alyssa, Jamie, Hannah, Kevin, Max, Casey, Chloe, Jack, and Lili Eva Bethel at Primlicious.com.

Scott, Michelle, Danielle, Tyler, and Morgan Bloyer.

Lori Rourke, hairdresser to the stars.

Jade Corn and Cori Ashley at Phoenix Book Company, and to Faith Hochhalter and all of the book club ladies and gents.

Treehouse Books, Anderson's Bookshop, Changing Hands Bookstore, and Kepler's.

My invisible friends who rock: Juliana, Ashlea, Cassie, Nicole, Chelsea, Melissa, and James Booth, and all the peeps at that one place who have given me so much support—you know who you are.

Jill Morgan at Flat Rock High School.

And to Vickie, Sahrie, Tashia, Nikki, and Katherine, the first five MySpace friends I met on book tour. You guys rock!

FADE

A NEW YEAR

January 1, 2006, 1:31 a.m.

Janie sprints through the snowy yards from two streets away and slips quietly through the front door of her house.

And then.

Everything goes black.

She grips her head, cursing her mother under her breath as the whirling kaleidoscope of colors builds and throws her off balance. She bumps against the wall and holds on, and then slowly lowers herself blindly to the floor as her fingers go numb. The last thing she needs is to crack her head open. Again.

She's too tired to fight it right now. Too tired to pull herself out of it. Plants her cheek on the cold tile floor. Gathers her strength so she can try later, in case the dream doesn't end quickly.

Breathes.

Watches.

1:32 a.m.

It's the same old dream Janie's mother always has. The one where a much younger, much happier mother flies through a psychedelic tunnel of flashing, spinning, colored lights, holding hands with the hippie who looks like Jesus Christ. Their sunglasses reflect the dizzying stripes, making it even harder for Janie to stop the vertigo.

This dream always makes Janie sick to her stomach.

What's her stupid mother doing sleeping in the living room, anyway?

But Janie is curious. She tries to focus. She peers at the man in the dream as she floats alongside the oblivious pair. Janie's mother could see Janie, if only she looked. But she never does.

The man can't see her, of course. It's not his dream. Janie wishes she could get him to take off his sunglasses. She wants to see his face. Wonders if his eyes are brown like hers. She can never focus her attention in one place for long, though, with all the spinning colors.

Abruptly the dream changes.

Sours.

The hippie man fades, and Janie's mother stands in a line of people that stretches on for what seems like miles. Her shoulders curl over, worn, like thin pages in a well-read book.

Her face is grim, set. Angry.

She's holding—

jiggling—

a screaming, red-faced baby.

Not this again. Janie doesn't want to watch anymore—she hates this part. Hates it. She gathers all her strength and concentrates. Hard. Groans inwardly. And pulls herself out of her mother's dream.

Exhausted.

1:51 a.m.

Janie's vision slowly returns. She shivers in a cold sweat and flexes her aching fingers, grateful that she never seems to get sucked back into a dream once she's successfully pulled out of it. So far, anyway.

She pushes herself to her feet as her mother snores on the couch, and walks shakily to the bathroom, stomach churning. She gags and retches, then makes a halfhearted attempt at brushing her teeth. Once in her bedroom, Janie closes the door tightly behind her.

Falls to the bed, like a lump of dough.

After last month's ordeal with the drug bust, Janie knows she's got to get her strength back or the dreams will take over her life again.

That night, Janie's own dreams are blasted with churning oceans and hurricanes and life jackets that sink like stones.

11:44 a.m.

Janie wakes to sunlight streaming in. She's ravenous and dreaming about food now. Smelling it.

"Cabe?" she mumbles, eyes closed.

"Hey. I let myself in." He sits on the bed next to her, his fingers drawing her tangled hair away from her face. "Rough night, Hannagan? Or are you still catching up?"

"Mrrff." She rolls over. Sees the plate of eggs and toast, steam rising. Grins wide as the ocean and lunges for it. "You—best secret boyfriend ever."

ASSIGNMENTS
AND SECRETS

January 2, 2006, 11:54 a.m.

It's the last day of winter break.

Janie and Cabel sit in Cabel's spare bedroom—his computer room—checking the school website for their exam grades.

It's a good thing Cabel has two laptops. Or there might be an all-out fight when the grades are posted at noon. But who are they kidding. They might have to roll around on the floor and wrestle, regardless.

Janie's nervous.

She turned in a blank blue book for the math exam after the drug bust went down a few weeks ago. She had a good excuse; there was still blood on her sweat-shirt, after all. And the teacher gave her a second shot at it. Too bad it was on the day after a rough night of dream-hopping at Fieldridge High's annual all-night fundraiser danceathon. Also too bad—it was a lock in. No escape.

Janie and Cabe might have skipped the whole dance if they could have, but it wasn't possible. They were on assignment.

Undercover.

Captain's orders.

"We're looking for anybody who dreams about teachers, Janie," Captain had said. "Or any teachers who are dreaming about students."

Janie thought that sounded odd and intriguing. "Anything specific?" she'd asked.

"Not at this time," Captain said. "I'll fill you in more after the New Year, once we've got some things sorted out. For now, just take notes of anything teacher/student related."

For Janie, staying up all night isn't the problem. It's the dream-hopping that sucks the life out of her. And after spending six hours stuck in other people's dreams from her hidden location under the bleachers, she was completely spent.

Of course Cabel was there, at the dance, slipping Janie cartons of milk and PowerBars (she'd reluctantly switched from Snickers). The dreams were on the fertile side, to say the least.

Too bad she didn't pick up anything substantial. Nothing teacher/student related. Only student/student related, to Janie's chagrin.

And when Luke Drake, the Fieldridge High football team's star receiver, fell asleep on the gymnastics mats, already totally plastered when he arrived at the lock in, Janie cried, "Enough."

"Cabe," she gasped between dreams, "wake him the fuck up, and don't let him sleep again. I can't take it."

Luke tends to dream about himself, and it turns out he's a bit overconfident when naked. Cabel's seen Luke in the showers after PE "Luke's definitely overcompensating in his dreams," Cabel says when he hears Janie's description.

Cabe may or may not have had more success in his assignment that night. He's a relationship builder, so his work takes more time than Janie's to see results. He makes connections, builds trust, and has the uncanny ability to get people to admit the most amazing things while bugged. And Janie plays cleanup. At least that's how beautifully it went the first time.

Needless to say, Janie knows she didn't ace the second

math exam either. And today, the last day before going back for their final semester at Fieldridge High, Janie's stressed about her grades.

She doesn't need to be.

She has a terrific scholarship.

But she's funny like that.

At noon exactly, according to Cabel's police scanner, they log on from their respective computers and scan their pages.

Janie sighs. Under different circumstances, it would have been an A. Math's her best subject. Which makes it all the worse.

Cabel's sensitive. He doesn't react to his row of straight As. He feels responsible for Janie's face-first free-fall at the police station that landed her in the hospital during exam week.

They simultaneously close their screens.

Not that they're competitive.

They aren't.

Okay, they are.

Cabel glances sidelong at Janie.

She looks away.

He changes the subject. "Time to go see Captain," he says.

Janie checks her watch and nods. "See you there."

Janie slips out of Cabe's house and runs across the yards of two small residential streets to her house. Janie looks around, sees no one, so she peeks into her mother's bedroom. Her mother is there, passed out but alive, bottles strewn about as usual. She's not dreaming, thank goodness. Janie closes the bedroom door softly, grabs her car keys, and heads back outside in the cold to start up Ethel.

Ethel is Janie's 1977 Nova. She bought the car from Stu Gardner, who has been dating Janie's best friend, Carrie Brandt, for two years. Stu's a mechanic. He babied Ethel from the time he was thirteen years old, and Janie respects the tradition. The car roars to life. Janie pats the dashboard appreciatively. Ethel hums.

Cabel and Janie arrive separately at the police station. They park in different locations. They enter the building using different doors. And they don't meet again until Janie gets to Captain's office. It's important that nobody sees them together until the drug case with Shay Wilder's father is closed, or else their duties with this new assignment could be compromised.

It's because Janie and Cabel work undercover as narcs at Fieldridge High School. Janie's discovering there are a lot of weird things that happen at her school. More than she could have ever imagined.

Cabel's already sitting there with Captain when Janie walks in. He hands out cups of coffee for the three of them. He stirs Janie's with a stir stick after having prepared it just the way she likes it: three creams, three sugars.

She needs the calories.

Because of all the dreams.

She's finally getting some padding and muscle back on her bones, after the last big thing.

Janie sits before she's ordered to sit.

"Nice to see you, Hannagan. You look better than the last time I saw you," remarks Captain in a gruff voice.

"Glad to see you too, sir," Janie says to the woman, Captain Fran Komisky. "You don't look so bad yourself, if I may say so." She hides a smile.

Captain raises an eyebrow. "You two are going to piss me off today, I can just feel it," she says. She runs her fingers through her short bronze hair, and adjusts her skirt. "Anything to report, Strumheller?"

"Not really, sir," Cabel says to her. "Just the usual schmoozing. Making the rounds. Trying to get a better picture of what some of the teachers and students are like outside the classroom."

Captain turns to Janie. "Anything from the dreams, Hannagan?"

"Nothing useful," Janie says. She feels bad.

Captain nods. "As I expected. This is going to be a tough one."

"Sir, if I may ask . . . ," Janie begins.

"You want to know what's going on." Captain rises abruptly, closes the door to her office, and returns to her desk, a serious look on her face.

"Last March, our Crimebusters Underground Quick Cash school program received a phone call on the Fieldridge High School line. You've heard of that program, right? All the schools in the area participate. Each school has its own line, so Crimebusters knows which school the complaint is from."

Cabel nods. "Students can earn a reward—fifty bucks, I think—if they report a crime directly related to schools. That's how we were tipped off about the drug parties on the Hill, Janers."

Janie nods. She's heard of it too. Has the hotline-number magnet on her refrigerator like everybody else in Fieldridge. "Hey, fifty bucks is fifty bucks. It's a smart program."

Captain continues. "Anyway. The caller didn't actually

say much of anything. It's very distant sounding—almost as if she dialed but didn't put the phone to her mouth. It's only about a five-second call before the caller hangs up. Here's the recording of it. Tell me what you hear."

Captain presses a button on a machine behind her. Cabel and Janie strain to make out the garbled words. The voice sounds very far away and music pounds behind it.

Janie furrows her brow and leans forward. Cabel shakes his head, puzzled. "Could you play it again?"

"I'll play it a few more times. Concentrate on the background noise, too. There are other people talking in the distance." Captain plays the short message several times more. She slows the tape and speeds it up, then reduces the background noise. Finally she reduces the voice of the caller until only the background noise remains.

"Anything, either of you?" Captain asks.

"It's impossible to understand a single word the caller's saying," Cabel says. "Nobody's screaming, nobody sounds upset. I heard laughter in the background. The music sounds like Mos Def. Janie?"

"I hear a guy's voice in the background saying 'Mister' something."

Captain nods. "I hear that too, Janie. That's the only word I can make out in the entire call.

"We didn't think much of this call—didn't spend

time on it. There was no information, no complaint, no report of a crime. But then in November, there was another call to Crimebusters Underground. And when I heard this one, I remembered the call you just heard. Listen."

Captain plays the new call. It's a woman's slurred voice, giggling uncontrollably and saying, *"I want my Quick Cash! Fieldridge . . . High. Fucking teachers . . . fucking students. Omigod—this can't—oops!"* More giggles and then the call ends abruptly. Captain plays it for them a few times more.

"Wow," Janie says.

Captain looks from Janie to Cabel. "Anything jump out at you?"

Cabel squints. "Fucking teachers, fucking students? Is that a slam on Fieldridge teachers and students, or is it, you know, literal?"

"The music in the background is similar to the first recording," Janie says.

"Right, Janie. That's what made me think of the first call when this one came in. And yes, Cabe, we're taking it literally until, and unless, we're proven wrong. This call gave us enough information to do something with it. My hunch, from what little we have here, is that Fieldridge High may have a sexual predator hiding in their hallways."

"Can't you find out who made the calls and ask them what's going on?" Janie asks.

"Well, that would be breaking the law, Janie. The whole purpose of Crimebusters Underground is that the calls are anonymous, to protect the person reporting the crime, and they must remain that way. The callers are assigned a code name by which their individual tip is identified. Later, they can use that code name to check on the case and claim their reward if they have managed to give Crimebusters Underground a usable lead."

"That makes sense," Janie says sheepishly.

"What have you done so far, Captain?" Cabel asks. "And," he says more cautiously, "what are you hoping we can do?" His voice, for the first time, sounds edgy. Janie glances sidelong at him with mild surprise. She didn't expect to see him so uncomfortable about an assignment.

"We've done complete background checks on all the teachers. Everyone comes up squeaky clean. And now we're stuck. Cabe, Janie, this is why I had you at the all-nighter. I'm looking for any information you can give me about Fieldridge teachers who might be sexual predators in their spare time. Are you up for the challenge? This one could be a bit dangerous. Hannagan, chances are, the predator is male. If we can determine who we're after, we may need to use you as bait so we can nail him. Think about it and get back to me on how you feel about it.

If you don't want to do this assignment, you're off the hook. No pressure."

Cabel sits up, even more concerned. "Bait? You're going to put her out there for the creep to prey on?"

"Only if she wants to."

"No way," Cabel says. "Janie, no. It's too dangerous."

Janie blinks and glares at Cabel. "Mom? Is that you?" She laughs nervously, not enjoying the confrontation. "What do you mean it's too dangerous?"

Captain interjects. "We'll have your back at all times, Janie. Besides, we don't know what's going on yet. It may be nothing. I'm hoping you can get at least some of the information we need through dreams."

Cabel shakes his head at Janie. "I don't like this."

Janie raises an eyebrow. "Right. Only you are allowed to do something dangerous. Jeez, Cabe. It's really not your decision."

Cabel looks at Captain for help.

Captain pointedly ignores him and looks at Janie.

"I don't need to think about it, sir. Count me in," Janie says.

"Good."

Cabel frowns.

Captain spends the next thirty minutes coaching them on the art of obtaining information. It's a refresher course for Cabel, who's been a narc for a year now (although Janie knows better than to call him that) and was responsible for the most recent Fieldridge drug bust of Shay Wilder's father, who had a gold mine of cocaine hidden on his boat. It was Janie who figured out the location of the cake when Mr. Wilder fell asleep in jail. She and Cabel make a good team.

And Captain knows it.

It's why she puts up with their shit—now and then.

Captain reiterates the assignment and encourages the two seniors to keep plugging away. "If we are dealing with a sexual predator, we need to nail the bastard before he hurts another Fieldridge student."

"Yes, sir," Janie says.

Cabel folds his arms over his chest and shakes his head, defeated. Finally says, "Yes, sir."

Captain nods and rises from her chair. Instinctively Cabel and Janie rise too. The meeting is over. But before they leave the office, Captain says, "Janie? I need to speak with you alone. Cabe, you may go."

Cabe doesn't hesitate. He's gone, without so much as a glance at Janie. Janie can't help puzzling over why Cabel's acting like he is.

Captain walks to a file cabinet and pulls out several thick files.

Janie stands in silence. Watching.

Wondering.

Captain still scares her some.

Because Janie's pretty new at this.

Finally, Captain returns to the desk with the stack of files and loose papers. Puts them in a box. Sits down. Looks at Janie.

"New topic. This is classified," Captain says. "You get what that means?"

Janie nods.

"Not even Cabe, right? You understand?"

Janie nods somberly. "Yes, sir," she adds.

Captain studies Janie for a moment, and then shoves the stack of files and papers toward Janie. "The reports. Twenty-two years worth of reports and notes. Written by Martha Stubin."

Janie's eyes grow wide. Fill with tears, despite her attempt to hold them back.

"You knew her, didn't you," Captain says, almost accusingly. "Why didn't you mention it? You had to know I'd do a full background check on you."

Janie doesn't know the answer Captain wants to hear. She only knows her own reasons. She hesitates, but then speaks. "Miss Stubin is . . . was . . . the only person who understood this—this stupid dream curse, and I didn't even know it until after she died," she says. She looks down at her lap. "I'm so bummed that I didn't have a chance to talk to her about it. And now all I have of her is an occasional cameo when she decides to show up in someone's dream, to show me how to do things." Janie swallows the lump in her throat. "She hasn't been around lately."

Captain Komisky is rarely at a loss for words. But she's showing signs of it now.

Finally she says, "Martha never mentioned you. She was searching. Hard. For her replacement. There were others like her, years ago, but they are gone now too. She must have only discovered you recently."

Janie nods. "I fell into one of her dreams at the nursing home. She talked to me in her dream, but I didn't understand that it was different with her—that she was testing me, teaching me. Not until after she died."

Then Captain says, "I think the only reason she lived as long as she did was because she was determined to find the next catcher. You."

There is a moment of warmth in the room.

And then it is back to business.

Captain clears her throat loudly and says, "Well. I expect there's some interesting stuff in here. Some of it might be tough. Take a month or so to read through it.

And if you find anything you don't understand or are worried about, you'll come talk to me. Is that clear?"

Janie looks at her. She has no idea what to expect from the files. But she does know what Captain expects to hear. "Sir, yes, sir," she says. With a confidence she doesn't feel.

Captain straightens the papers on her desk, indicating that the meeting is over. Janie stands up abruptly and takes the stack of files. "Thank you, sir," Janie says, and heads out the door.

She doesn't see Captain Fran Komisky watching her go, thoughtfully tapping her chin with a pen, after Janie closes the door behind her.

Janie drives home, happy to see the few rays of sunshine forcing their way through the gray clouds on this cold January afternoon. But she's feeling an ominous presence emanating from the pile of materials Captain gave her, and an unsettled feeling about Cabel's strange reaction to the assignment. She stops at her house, makes quick eye contact with her mother, and dumps the literature on her bed.

She'll deal with it later.

But now, she's dying to spend her last vacation day with Cabel.

Before they have to go back to the real world of school.

And pretend they're not in love.

4:11 p.m.

Janie sprints through the yards, taking a different path to Cabel's this time. She can't be seen by anyone connected to her high school. But the good thing is that almost nobody who matters at Fieldridge High lives anywhere near the poor side of town.

Still, Janie doesn't leave her car at Cabel's. Just in case Shay Wilder drives by.

Because Shay's still hot for Cabe.

And Shay has no clue that Cabel busted her dad for drugs.

It's sort of funny.

But not really.

Janie comes in through the back door now, to be safe. She has a key. In case Cabel goes to bed before she can get there. But lately, since she quit her job at Heather Nursing Home, she has more time than ever to spend with Cabel.

They have an unusual relationship.

And when things are good, it's magic.

She closes the door behind her, taking off her shoes. Wonders where he is. Tiptoes around, in case he's grabbing a nap, but he's nowhere on the tiny main floor. Opens the door to the basement and sees the light is flicked on.

She pads down the stairs, and pauses on the bottom step, watching him. Admiring him.

She whips off her sweatshirt and tosses it on the step. Presses up against the metal support beam, stretching her arms, her back, her legs. Wanting to be strong and sexy, too. She lets her hair fall forward over her face as she concentrates on stretching.

He sees her and sets the weight bar in its cradle. Stands up. His muscles ripple under the spread of nubbly burn scars on his stomach and chest. He's narrow and gangly and muscular. Not beefy. Just right. And Janie's really happy that he doesn't seem uncomfortable without a shirt on in her presence anymore.

Janie has an urge to attack him right there on the weight bench. But after all they'd been through together in such a short time, neither of them wants to mess up the relationship on the sex end of things. And Cabel, conscious enough of his many burn scars, isn't quite ready to show off the ones below the belt. So Janie admires him from five feet away instead. And hopes he's gotten over his issues about Janie helping with this case.

"Your eyes are bright again," he says. "It's good to see you rested. And your scar is wicked sexy." He picks up his towel and wipes the sweat off his face, then rubs the towel over his honey-brown hair. A few damp strands travel down his neck. He walks up to her and moves her hair away from her face, getting a good look at the inch-long scar under her eyebrow that is now healing nicely. "God," he murmurs. "You're gorgeous." He plants a gentle kiss on her lips, and then he towels off his chest and back, and slips on his T-shirt.

Janie blinks. "Are you high?" She laughs, self-conscious. She's still not accustomed to attention, much less compliments.

He leans in and runs a finger lightly from her ear, across her jaw line, down her neck. Her heart pounds and she closes her eyes inadvertently, sucking in a breath. He takes advantage of her distraction and begins to nibble on her neck. He smells like Axe and fresh sweat, and it's making her crazy. She reaches for him. Pulls him close. Feels the heat from his skin blasting through his shirt.

It's the touching they both long for.

The holding.

Spent their whole lives, each without any. Figure it's time to make up for it.

Cabel hands her the weight bar.

"So . . . ," Janie says carefully. "You feeling better about me doing this, uh, bait thing?"

"Not really."

"Oh." She lowers the bar to her chest and presses upward.

"I don't want you doing it."

Janie concentrates and presses again. "Why? What's your problem?" she huffs.

"I just . . . don't like it. You could get hurt. Raped. My God . . ." he trails off. His jaw is set. "I can't let you do it. Say no."

Janie sets the bar in the cradle and sits up, her eyes flashing. "It's not your decision, Cabe."

Cabel sighs deeply and rakes his fingers through his hair. "Janie—"

"What? You think I can't handle the job? You can go out and mess with dangerous drug dealers and spend nights in jail, but I can't get involved in anything dangerous? What kind of a double standard is that?" She stands up and faces him.

Looks him in the eye.

His brown silky eyes plead back at hers. "This is different," he says weakly.

"Because you can't control it?"

Cabel sputters. "No—It's just—"

Janie grins. "You are so busted. Better get used to the idea. I'm in for the ride on this one."

Cabel looks at her a minute more. Closes his eyes and slowly hangs his head. Sighs. "I still don't like it. I can't stand the thought of any sicko teacher anywhere near you."

Janie wraps her arms around his neck. Rests her head against his shoulder. "I'll be careful," she whispers.

Cabel is silent.

He presses his lips into her hair and squeezes his eyes shut. "Why can't you just be the one safe thing in my life?" he whispers.

Janie pulls away and looks up at him.

Smiles sympathetically.

"Because safe equals boring, Cabe."

Janie spends almost an hour lifting weights. Three weeks, Cabel says, and she'll start to see the changes. All she knows is that her glutes are killing her.

6:19 p.m.

Janie and Cabel step on each other's feet in the small kitchen as they broil fish in the oven and fix a mountain of veggies. Cabel is a healthy eater. And he insists Janie eats that way too. Now that she's lost so much weight. Now that he realizes what she's in for, for the rest of her life. "It makes me crazy, seeing you so thin like that, you know," he murmurs as he checks the salmon. "And not in a good way."

At night, on the nights she stays over, he massages her aching fingers and toes before she drifts off to sleep. Falling into one nasty nightmare will do that to her—leave her fingers numb and aching for hours after. Cabel, having learned recently to control his dreams to some extent, has made dream control into a religion. He spends an hour a day in meditation, talking himself into calm, sweet dreams, working his way to his ideal—no dreams at all. At least when Janie's over. So he can keep her nearby. He's managed to prevent himself from dreaming one entire night now—with Janie as his witness. She woke up so refreshed, he hardly knew her.

That's another reason why this new assignment is putting him on edge. He knows the dreams will make this harder on her than on him.

Physically, anyway.

Mentally? Emotionally? It'll be harder on him.

Because this love thing is foreign to Cabel. And now that he has found Janie, he's becoming increasingly protective of her. There is no man in the universe he wants to have to share her with. Especially a creep.

Even if it unearths a scandal.

Of greatest proportions.

The biggest scandal Fieldridge High has ever seen.

10:49 p.m.

Janie stays over.

"Are we okay?" she asks softly.

After a silence, Cabel whispers, "We're okay."

He wraps his arms around her in bed, and they talk quietly, like usual.

Janie brings it up first. "So, spill it. All As, right?"

He squeezes her. Closes his eyes. "Yeah."

"I got a B+ in math," she finally says.

He's quiet. Not quite sure what she wants to hear. Maybe she just wants to say it and be done. Get it out there, so it can float away and not be so painful.

He waits a moment. And then murmurs, "I love you, Janie Hannagan. I can't get enough of you. I wake up in the morning and all I want to do is be with you." He props himself up on his elbow. "Do you have any idea how unusual, how important that is to me? Compared to some stupid test you took under extreme duress, twice?"

He said it.

It's the first time he said it out loud.

Janie swallows. Hard.

Understands what he means, completely.

Wants to tell him how she feels about him.

Problem is, Janie can't remember saying "I love you" to anyone. Ever.

She burrows closer into him. How could she have gone so many years without touching people? Hugs? Arms wrapped loosely in slumber, like a tired Christmas package whose ribbon hangs on, even until the last moment.

They confirm their plans for tomorrow under the covers. Opposite schedules unlike last semester, because they need to make a broader canvas through the school. All different teachers, too. This time Cabel set up his schedule with Principal Abernethy after Janie got hers, without Abernethy knowing why he picked the classes, teachers, and times that he chose. Principal Abernethy knows about Cabel's job. But he doesn't know about Janie's, and Captain wants to keep it that way.

Cabel agreed with the schedule setup, except for one thing. His only insistence with Captain was to have study hall at the same time as Janie. So he can cover for her, in case anybody ever sees what happens to her in there. Captain agreed.

Last semester, Janie and Cabel had identical schedules. Which Cabel insists was a fluke.

Janie doesn't believe him.

Or maybe she wants to believe that he found her on purpose. Even Janie can have her dreams.

They drift off to sleep. And when Cabel starts to dream, she startles awake, fights it off, and slides away from him, closes his door, and finishes her night's rest on the couch.

January 3, 2006, 6:50 a.m.

She wakes up to the smell of bacon and coffee. Her stomach growls, but it's normal hunger, not the famished, about-to-pass-out feeling she sometimes has after a night of falling into others' nightmares.

Janie doesn't want to open her eyes, and then he's there, on top of her and her blankets, kissing her ear. "Next time, kick me out of the bed," he whispers. The weight of him feels amazing on her body.

Maybe it's because she's numb so often.

Or because she was so numb inside, before she let him in.

She opens her eyes slowly. It takes her a moment to adjust to the bright kitchen light, shining in her eyes. "Can we rearrange the furniture this weekend?" she asks sleepily. "So when I sleep out here, you don't shine all of Satan's fiery hell lights in my eyes first thing in the morning?"

"Awww. Don't be grumpy. We're going into the best time of our lives. Be excited!"

He's joking.

Everyone who is heading to college knows that the best semester comes in four more years. Although this one will probably be easier.

Awake now, she shoves him off her, even though she'd rather lie like this all day. "Shower," she mumbles, shuffling off in that direction. Her muscles ache from working out. But it's a good ache.

When she emerges, breakfast is on the table.

She's finally gotten used to eating here, at this table.

After Cabel's nightmare about the knives and all.

And then she has to go.

Back to her house to check on her mother and get her car.

She clings to him.

She doesn't understand why.

Except it makes her happy.

He kisses her.

She kisses him.

They kiss.

And then she goes.

Out the door, crunching through the crust on eighteen inches of Michigan snow. Runs into her house. Makes sure her mother has food in the fridge. And grabs money for lunch.

She and Cabel accidentally park near each other at school, which makes Ethel very happy, Janie thinks.

7:53 a.m.

Carrie whaps Janie on the back of the head. "Hey, *chica*," she says, her eyes dancing, as usual. "I've hardly seen you over the holiday break. You all better?"

Janie grins. "I'm good. Check out my cool-ass scar."

Carrie whistles, impressed.

"How's Stu? Did you have a good Christmas?"

"Well, after the whole jail experience, I was pretty bummed out for a few days, but hey, shit happens. We had our court thingy yesterday, and I did what you suggested. I got my charges dropped, but Stu had to pay a fine. No jail time, though. It was a good thing he didn't do any coke." She whispers this last bit.

"Good job." Janie grins. She knew Carrie's drug charges would be dropped. She just couldn't tell her that.

"Oh, that reminds me," Carrie continues. She digs around in her backpack and pulls out an envelope. "Here's your college money back," she says. "Thanks again, Janie. You were awesome to come out in the middle of the night to bail us out. So, what's the deal with your seizures, anyway? That really freaked me out."

Janie blinks. Carrie-speak is almost always at full-speed, and it changes direction often. Which is okay. Because Janie can usually dodge any questions she doesn't want to answer without Carrie noticing.

Carrie is a little self-centered.

And immature at times.

But she's the only girlfriend Janie's got, and they're both loyal as hell.

"Oh, you know." Janie yawns. "The doc's gotta run some tests and stuff. Made me take off work from the nursing home for a while. But if you ever see me do that again—have a seizure, I mean—don't worry. Just make sure I don't fall and crack open my skull on a rusty coffee cart next time, will you?"

Carrie shudders. "Gah, don't talk about it!" she says. "You're giving me the heebs. Hey, I heard Cabel's in some deep shit with the cops over this whole cocaine scandal. Have you seen him? I wonder if he's still in jail."

Janie's eyes widen. "No way! You think? Let me know what you find out from Melinda and Shay."

"Of course." Carrie grins.

Carrie loves a good scandal.

And Janie loves Carrie. Wishes she didn't have to keep secrets from her.

2:25 p.m.

Janie and Cabel have study hall last period in the school library. They don't sit together. Nobody looks sleepy. Things are going smoothly.

Janie, tucked away at her favorite table in the far back corner of the library, finishes a boring English lit assignment and then tackles her Chem. 2 homework. Her first impression of that class is positive. Only a few geeks take it—it's a college-credit course. But Janie, having satisfied all her required courses, is taking whatever she can to help her out in college. Advanced math, Spanish, Chemistry 2, and psychology. Psychology is a Captain requirement. "It's crucial to police work," she'd said. "Especially the kind of work you'll be doing."

A paper wad lands on Janie's page of homework and bounces to the ground. Janie picks it up while still reading her text book, and opens it up, pressing out the wrinkles.

4:00 p.m.?

That's what the note says.

Janie glances casually to the left, between two rows of bookshelves, and nods.

2:44 p.m.

Janie's chemistry book thumps to the table as everything goes dark.

She lays her head on her arms as she gets sucked into a dream.

For crap's sake! thinks Janie. It's Cabel's dream. It figures.

Janie goes along for the ride, although normally she tries to pull out of his dreams now that his nightmares have quieted. But, ever curious, she rides this one out, knowing the bell will ring soon, ending the school day.

Cabel is rummaging through his closet, methodically putting on shirts and sweaters over one another, layering more and more pieces until he can hardly move his blimplike body.

Janie doesn't know what to think. Feeling invasive, she pulls herself out of the dream.

When she can see again, she stacks her books into her backpack and waits, thoughtful, until the bell rings.

4:01 p.m.

Janie slips in the back door of Cabel's house, shakes the snow off her boots, and leaves them inside the heated wooden box next to the door. She folds her coat and sets it next to the boots, and heads to the basement.

"Hey," grunts Cabel from the bench press.

Janie grins. She stretches out her slightly aching muscles, picks up the ten-pound barbells, and begins with squats.

They work out in silence for forty-five minutes.

Both of them are mentally reviewing the day.

They'll talk about it—soon.

5:32 p.m.

Showered and settled at the small, round conference table in the computer room, Cabel pulls out a sheet of paper and a pen while Janie fires up the laptop.

"Here's what your profile sheets should look like," he says, sketching. "I e-mailed you the template."

Cabel points out the various columns, explaining in full as to what sort of information should be written in each one. Janie pulls up the template on her screen, squints and then frowns, and fills in the first one.

"Why are you squinting?"

"I'm not. I'm concentrating."

Cabel shrugs.

"Okay, so first hour is Miss Gardenia, Spanish, room 112, and the list of students. You want their real names or Spanish names?" Janie looks at him, deadpan.

He grins and pulls her hair.

She types quickly.

Like, ninety words a minute.

She uses all of her fingers, not just one from each hand.

Imagine that.

Cabel gawks. "Holy shit. Will you do mine for me?"

"Sure. But you'll have to dictate. Going back and forth between computer screen and handwritten notes gives me a headache. And it makes me very cranky."

"How did you . . . ?" He knows she doesn't own a computer.

"Nursing home," she says. "Files, files, files. Charts,

records, transcribing medical terms, prescriptions, all that."

"Wow."

"Why don't we do yours first. Then I'll have a better understanding of how to do mine."

Cabel flips through a spiral notebook. "Okay," he says. "I already scribbled some notes here, at school—No! Not the evil eyebrow! I'll decipher them and dictate, I promise."

Janie glances at his notes.

"What the . . . ," she says, and grabs the notebook.

Reads the page.

Looks at him.

"Mr. Green, Mrs. White, Miss Scarlet . . . Well, if it isn't Professor Plum. So where the hell is Colonel Mustard?" She bursts out laughing.

"Colonel Mustard is Principal Abernethy," he says with a sniff.

Janie stops laughing.

Sort of.

Actually, she giggles every few minutes as she reads. Especially when she finds out Miss Scarlet is actually Mr. Garcia, the industrial tech teacher.

"It's coded for secrecy, Janie." He's really not sounding amused. "In case I lose the notebook, or somebody looks over my shoulder."

Janie stops mocking him.

But he continues. "It's a smart idea. You should

code your notes too, if you take any. It only takes one stupid mistake to blow your cover. And then we're all screwed."

Janie waits.

Makes sure he's finished.

Then says, "You're right. I'm sorry, Cabe."

He looks mildly redeemed.

"All right then, moving on," he says. "First hour is advanced math. Mr. Stein. Room 134."

She plugs in the info, including the class list. "Anything of note?" she asks.

"In this space here," he says, pointing, "write, 'slight German accent, tendency to trip over words when excited, constantly fidgets with chalk.' The guy's a nervous wreck," Cabel explains.

"Next is Mrs. Pancake." They don't chuckle at the name, because they've known her for years now. "I have nothing of note on her. She's just that sweet, round grandma type—not the profile I expect we'll be after, but we don't rule anybody out, okay? I'll keep watching."

Janie nods and goes to the third page, fills in the appropriate information, and within thirty minutes, Cabel's charts are done for the day. She e-mails them to him.

"I'm going to finish my homework while you're working on your charts, if you don't mind," he says. "Let me know if you have any questions. And be sure to take notes of any intuition, funny feelings, suspicions—anything. There are no wrong things to track."

"Got it," Janie says. She clicks her fingers over the keyboard with finesse, and finishes her charts before Cabel gets his homework done. She goes back and lingers over each entry, trying to think of anything of note, and promises herself to be more discerning tomorrow.

"So," she says lightly when Cabel closes his books, "did you talk to Shay today?" Janie couldn't help noticing Shay was in three of his classes.

Cabel looks at her with a small smile. Knows what she's really asking. "The thought of being with Shay Wilder makes me want to gouge my eyes out with a butter knife," he says. He pulls Janie toward him in a half-hug. She rests her head on his shoulder, and he smoothes her hair. "Are you staying tonight?" He asks after a while. There's hope in his voice.

Janie thinks about the box of files from Captain on her bed.

She hates that they're sitting there, untouched. It's like homework hanging over her head. She can't stand it.

But.

She also hates the thought of leaving Cabel.

The question hangs in the air.

"I can't," she says finally. "I've got some things to do at home."

It's hard, somehow, to say good-bye tonight. They linger near the back door, forehead to forehead and curved like statues as their lips whisper and brush together.

9:17 p.m.

Janie comes home to a mess after getting stuck hiding in a stand of trees for fifteen minutes while Carrie shoveled snow off her car and left, probably off to Stu's apartment. Janie doesn't want any questions about where she was coming from. She knows the day will inevitably come where Carrie discovers Janie's car in the driveway but Janie not home.

Luckily, Stu and Carrie spend most of their time together. Carrie's parents like him all right. Even after Carrie broke down and told them she'd been arrested. They seemed relieved to hear that Stu wasn't into cocaine.

Of course, they still grounded Carrie. For life. As usual.

9:25 p.m.

Janie settles in her bed under the covers, and opens the box of material from Captain. She pulls out the first file, and dives into Miss Stubin's life.

News flash: Miss Stubin never taught school.

And she was married.

Janie's jaw hangs open for two hours. The frail, gnarled, blind, stick-thin, former school teacher who Janie read books to lived a secret life.

11:30 p.m.

Janie holds her aching head. Closes the file. Returns the stack to the cardboard box and hides it in her closet. Then she turns out her light and slips back under the covers.

Thinks about the military man in Miss Stubin's dream.

Miss Stubin, thinks Janie as a grin turns on her lips, *was a player back in the day.*

1:42 a.m.

Janie dreams in black and white.

She's walking down Center Street at dusk. The weather is cool and rainy. Janie's been here before, although she doesn't know what town she's in. She looks around excitedly at the corner by the dry goods store, but there is no young couple there, strolling arm in arm.

"I'm here, Janie," comes a soft voice from behind. "Come, sit with me."

Janie turns around and sees Miss Stubin seated in her wheelchair next to a park bench along the street.

"Miss Stubin?"

The blind old woman smiles. "Ah, good. Fran has given you my notes. I've been hoping for you."

Janie sits on the park bench, her heart thumping. She feels tears spring to her eyes and quickly blinks them away. "It's good to see you again, Miss Stubin." Janie slips her hand into Miss Stubin's gnarled fingers.

"Yes, there you are, indeed." Miss Stubin smiles. "Shall we get on with it, then?"

Janie's puzzled. "Get on with it?"

"If you are here, then you must have agreed to work with Captain Komisky, as I did."

"Does Captain know I'm having this dream?" Janie is confused.

Miss Stubin chuckles. "Of course not. You may tell her if you wish. Give her my fond regards. But I'm here to fulfill a promise to myself. To be available to you, just as the one who taught me remained with me until I was fully prepared, fully knowledgeable about what my purpose was in life. I'm here to help you as best as I can, until you no longer need me."

Janie's eyes grow wide. *No!* she thinks, but she doesn't say it. She hopes it takes a very long time before she no longer needs Miss Stubin.

"We'll meet here from time to time as you go through my case files. When you have questions about my notes, return here. I trust you know how to find me again?"

"You mean, direct myself to dream this again?"

Miss Stubin nods.

"Yes, I think I can do that. I'm sort of out of practice," Janie says sheepishly.

"I know you can, Janie." The old woman's curled fingers tighten slightly around Janie's hand. "Do you have an assignment from Captain?"

"Yes. We think there's a teacher who is a sexual predator at Fieldridge High."

Miss Stubin sighs. "Difficult. Be careful. And be creative—It may be tricky to find the right dreams to fall into. Keep up your strength. Be prepared for every opportunity to search out the truth. Dreams happen in the strangest places. Watch for them."

"I—I will," Janie says softly.

Miss Stubin cocks her head to the side. "I must go now." She smiles and fades away, leaving Janie alone on the bench.

2:27 a.m.

Janie's eyes flutter and open. She stares at the ceiling in the dark, and then flips on her bedside lamp. Scribbles the dream in her notebook. *Wow*, she thinks. *Cool*.

Grins sleepily as she turns out the light and rolls over, back to sleep.

POINTED VIEWS

January 6, 2006, 2:10 p.m.

Janie codes her notes now, too:

Bashful=Spanish, Miss Gardenia
Doc=Psychology, Mr. Wang
Happy=Chemistry 2, Mr. Durbin
Dopey=English Lit., Mr. Purcell
Dippy=Math, Mrs. Craig
Dumbass=PE, Coach Crater

And, of course, Sleepy=Study hall

There's definitely something sleepy about Michigan in its darkest months of January and February.

Study hall is a disaster. And after relatively few incidents, besides Cabel's dreams, over the past few weeks, Janie's feeling the pull harder than ever.

She needs to practice concentrating at home, in her own dreams again. Stay strong, like Miss Stubin told her in the dream. Or else she's going down.

2:17 p.m.

Janie feels it coming. She sets her book down and glances at Cabel. It's not him. He gives her a pitying half-smile when he sees the look on her face, and she tries to smile back. But it's too late.

It hits her, like a bag of rocks to the gut, and she doubles over in her chair, blinded, her mind whirling into Stacey O'Grady's dream. Janie recognizes it—Stacey was in Janie's study hall last semester too, and had this same nightmare a few months ago.

Janie is in Stacey's car, and Stacey is driving like a maniac down a dark street near the woods. From the backseat, a growl, and then a man appears and grabs Stacey around the neck from behind. Stacey's choking. She loses control of the car, and it careens over a ditch, smashes into a line of bushes, and flips over.

The man is shaken loose of his grasp, and when the car comes to rest in a parking lot, Stacey, bleeding, climbs out of the car through the broken windshield and starts running. He gets out and follows her. It's a mad chase, and Janie is swept into it. She can't concentrate hard enough to get Stacey's attention, and Stacey is screaming at the top of her lungs. Around and around the parking lot, the man chases her, until she runs for the woods . . .

. . . trips

. . . falls

. . . and he is on top of her, pinning her down, growling, like a dog, in her face—

2:50 p.m.

Janie feels her muscles still twitching three minutes after it's over. She didn't hear the bell ring, but Stacey did, apparently, because the dream stopped abruptly.

Janie still can't feel anything. She can't see. But she can hear Cabel next to her. "It's okay, baby," he whispers. "It's gonna be okay."

2:57 p.m.

Cabel's gently rubbing her fingers. He's still whispering, letting her know no one is around, they've all left, and it's all going to be okay.

She sits up slowly.

Squeezes her hands till they ache with pain and plea-sure. Wiggles her toes. Her face feels like she's been to the dentist for a filling.

He's rubbing her shoulders, her arms, her temples. She stops shaking. Tries to speak. It comes out like a hiss.

3:01 p.m.

"Cabel," she finally says.

"You ready to try to move?" His voice is concerned.

She shakes her head slowly. Turns toward him. Reaches out. "I can't see yet," she says quietly. "How long has it been?"

Cabel moves his hands over her shoulders and back down to her fingers. "Not that long," he says softly. "A few minutes." *More like twelve.*

"That was a bad one."

"Yeah. Did you try to pull out of it?"

Janie rests her forehead on the heel of her hand and rolls her head slowly, side to side. Her voice is weak. "I didn't try to get out. I tried to help her change it. Couldn't get her to pay any attention to me."

Cabel paces.

They wait.

Slowly Janie can make out shapes. The world fades back in. "Phew," she says. Smiles shakily.

"I'm driving you home," Cabel says as the janitor

comes into the library, eyeing them suspiciously. Cabel shoves Janie's books into her backpack, a grim look on his face. He searches around in the pack and comes up empty-handed. "Don't you carry anything with you? I'm out of PowerBars."

"Um . . ." Janie bites her lip. "I'm okay now. I'll be fine. I can drive."

He scowls. Doesn't respond. Helps her stand up, slings her backpack over his shoulder, and they walk out to the parking lot. It's lightly snowing.

He opens the passenger-side door of his car and looks at her, his jaw set.

Patient.

Waiting.

Until she gets in.

He drives in silence through the snow to a nearby mini-mart, goes in, and returns with pint of milk and a plastic bag. "Open your backpack," he says.

She does it.

He pours half a dozen PowerBars into it. Opens a bar and hands it to her with the milk. "I'll get your car later," he says, holding his hand out for her keys. She looks down. Then hands them over.

He drives her to her house.

Stares at the steering wheel, his jaw set.

Waits for her to get out.

She glances at him, a puzzled expression on her face. "Oh," she says finally. She swallows the lump in her throat. Takes her backpack and the milk and gets out of the car. Closes the door. Goes up the steps and kicks the snow off her shoes. Not looking back.

He pulls out of the driveway slowly, making sure Janie gets inside okay. And drives away.

Janie goes to bed, confused and sad, and takes a nap.

8:36 p.m.

She's awake. Starving. Looks around the house for something healthy and finds a tomato, growing soft in the refrigerator. There's a tuft of mold on the stem. She sighs. There's nothing else. She shrugs on her coat and slips on her boots, grabs fifty dollars from the grocery envelope, and starts walking.

The snow is beautiful. Flakes so tiny they sparkle, sequins in the oncoming headlights and under street lamps. It's cold, maybe twenty degrees out. Janie slips on her mittens and secures her coat at her throat. Glad she wore boots.

When she reaches the grocery store a mile away, it's quiet inside. A few shoppers stroll to the Muzak piping from the speakers. The store is bright with yellowy light, and Janie squints as she enters. She grabs a cart and heads to the produce section, shaking the snowflakes from her hair as she walks. She loosens her coat and tucks her mittens in her pockets.

Shopping, once Janie actually gets there, is relaxing to her. She takes her time, reading labels, thinking about things that seem like they might taste good together, picking out the best vegetables, mentally calculating the total cost as she goes along. It's like therapy. By the time she's spent her approximate allotment, she slips through the baking aisle to get to the checkout. As she meanders, looking at the different kinds of oils and spices, she slows her cart.

Glances to the left.

Recalculates what's in her cart.

And hesitantly picks out a red box and a small round container. Puts them in the cart next to the eggs and milk.

She wheels to the front of the store and stands in a short line at the one lonely check-out counter. Janie glances at the periodicals while she waits. Rides through a wave of hunger nausea. Loads her things onto the belt and watches the scanner anxiously as the number creeps upward.

"Your total comes to fifty-two twelve."

Janie closes her eyes for a moment. "I'm sorry," she says. "I have exactly fifty dollars. I need to put something back."

The checker sighs. The line behind Janie grows. She flushes and doesn't look at any of them. Decides what's necessary.

Hesitantly picks out the cake mix and the frosting.

Hands them to the checker. "Take these off, please," she says quietly. *It figures*, she thinks.

The checker makes like this is huge deal. Stomps on the buttons with her fingers.

People thaw, drip, and shift on their feet behind Janie.

She ignores them.

Sweating profusely.

"48.01," the checker finally announces. She counts out the $1.99 in change like it's breaking her back to lift so many coins at once.

Janie strings the pregnant bags over her arms, three on each side, and flees. Sucks in the cold fresh air. Pumps her arms once she reaches the road to get in her workout for the day, trying not to crush the eggs and bread. Her arms ache pleasantly at first. Then they just plain ache.

After a quarter mile a car slows and comes to a stop in front of Janie. A man gets out. "Ms. Hannagan, isn't it?" he says. It's Happy. Also known as Mr. Durbin, her Chem. 2 teacher. "You need a ride? I was a few customers behind you in line."

"I'm . . . I'm okay. I like the walk," she says.

"You sure?" He flashes a skeptical smile. "How far are you going?"

"Just, you know. Up the hill a ways." Janie gestures with a nod of her head up the snowy road that disappears into the darkness beyond Mr. Durbin's headlights. "It's not that far."

"It's really no trouble. Get in." Mr. Durbin stands there, waiting, arm draped over the top of the open car door, like he won't take no for an answer. Which makes Janie's skin prickle. But . . . maybe she should take the chance to get to know Mr. Durbin a little better, for investigation purposes.

"Well . . ." Janie's starting to get shaky with hunger. "Thanks," she says, opening the passenger-side door. He slips back inside the car and moves four or five plastic grocery bags to the backseat, and she gets in. "Straight ahead, right on Butternut. Sorry," she adds. She's not sure why. For the inconvenience, maybe.

"Seriously, no problem. I live just across the viaduct on Sinclair," he says. "It's right on my way." The blast of the car heater fills the silence. "So, how do you like the class? I was happy to see so many students. Ten is big for this one."

"I like it," she says. It's Janie's favorite class, actually. But there's no need for him to know that. "I like the small size," she adds, after more silence, "because we each get our own lab station. In Chem. 1, we were always doubled up."

"Yep," he says. "Did you have Mrs. Beecher for Chem. 1?"

Janie nods. "Yeah."

Mr. Durbin pulls into the driveway when she points it out, and looks puzzled to see Janie's car standing there, looking like it's just been driven. There's no snow built up on it, and steam rises off the hood. "So, you prefer to walk on a frigid night like this and lug all that junk home through the snow?" He laughs.

She grins. "I wasn't sure I'd have ol' Ethel back tonight. Looks like she's here now." She doesn't explain further. He puts the car in park and opens his door. "Can I give you a hand?"

The bags, once she got into the car, had slipped every which way, and are now a tangled mess. "You don't need to do that, Mr. Durbin."

He hops out and hurries to her side of the car. "Please," he says. He gathers three bags and scoots out of her way, then follows her to the door.

Janie hesitates, knocking the snow off her boots, adjusting her bags, so she can open the door. Notices things about her house that she overlooks most days. Screen door with a rip in it and hanging a little bit loose on its hinges. Wood exterior rotting at the base, paint peeling from it.

Awkward, Janie thinks, going inside, Durbin at her heels. She flips on the entrance light and is momentarily blinded by the brightness. She stops in her tracks until she can see again, and Mr. Durbin bumps into her.

"Excuse me," he says, sounding embarrassed.

"My fault," she says, feeling a little creeped out by having him in the house. She's on her guard. Who knows? It could be him they're after.

They turn the corner into the shadowy kitchen. She puts her bags on the counter, and he sets his next to hers.

"Thank you."

He smiles. "No problem. See you Monday." He waves and heads back outside.

Monday. Janie's eighteenth birthday.

She rummages through the bags on a mission. Grabs a handful of grapes, rinses them off quickly, and shoves them in her mouth, craving the fructose rush. She starts to put things away when she hears a step behind her.

She whirls around. "Jesus, Cabe. You scared the crap out of me."

He dangles her car keys. "I let myself in. Thought you'd be here. Heard an extra voice, so I hid in your room. So, who was that?" he asks. He's trying to sound nonchalant. Failing miserably.

"Are you jealous?" Janie teases.

"Who. Was. It." He's enunciating.

She raises her eyebrow. "Mr. Durbin. He saw me walking home and asked if I wanted a ride. He was in line behind me at the store."

"That's Durbin?"

"Yes. It was very nice of him, I thought." Janie's gut thinks otherwise, but she's not feeling like having a work discussion with Cabel right now.

"He's . . . young. What's he doing, picking up students? That's odd."

Janie waits to see what his point is. But there doesn't seem to be one. Still, she makes a mental note to record this incident in her case notebook—can't be too cautious. Janie turns and continues to put things away. She's still confused over how quiet Cabel was earlier. Doesn't say anything.

"I didn't know where you were," he says finally.

"Well, if I knew you were coming, I would have left a note. However," she continues coolly, "I was under the impression that you were pissed at me. So I didn't expect I'd see you." She's visibly shaking by now, and grabs the milk, rips open the cap, and chugs from the bottle. She sets it down and looks for something that won't take long to prepare. She grabs a few more grapes and snarfs them.

He's watching her. There's a look in his eye, and she doesn't understand it.

"Thanks for bringing my car. I really appreciate it. Did you walk all the way back to school?"

"No. My brother Charlie gave me a lift."

"Well, thank him for me."

She's got the peanut butter open now, and globs it on to a piece of bread. She pours some of the milk into a tall glass, grabs the sandwich, and slips past Cabel into the living room. Flips on the TV and squints at it. "You want a sandwich or something?" she asks. "Would you like to stay?" She doesn't know what else to say. He's just looking at her.

Finally he pulls a piece of paper from his jacket pocket. Unfolds it. Turns off the TV. "Humor me for a minute," he says.

He stands directly in front of her, then turns and walks fifteen paces in the opposite direction. Stops and turns to face her again.

"What the hell are you doing?"

"Read this. Out loud, please."

It's an eye chart.

"Dude, I'm totally trying to eat, here."

"Read. Please."

She sighs and looks at the chart.

"*E,*" she says. And smirks.

He's not laughing.

She reads the next line.

And the one after that. Squinting. And guessing.

"Cover your right eye and do it again," he says.

She does it.

"Now cover your left."

"Grrr," she says. But does it.

By memory.

All she can make out with her right eye is the *E*. She doesn't say anything. Just says the letters she remembers from before.

And then he takes a second, different chart out.

"Do that eye again," he says.

"What is the deal with you?" she almost yells. "Jeez, Cabel. I'm not your little kid or something."

"Can you read it or not?"

"*N,*" she says.

"Is that as much as you can read?"

"Yeah."

"Okay." He bites his lip. "Excuse me for a minute, will you?"

"Whatever," she says. So she needs glasses—maybe. Big deal. Cabel disappears into her bedroom, and she hears him pacing over the creak in the floor and talking to himself.

Janie eats her sandwich and downs the glass of milk. Goes into the kitchen and makes another. Grabs a carrot and peels it over the garbage can. Pours another glass of milk.

Takes her feast to the living room again and sits down. Turns the TV back on. She's feeling much better. Her hands have stopped shaking. She swallows the last drops of milk and feels it sloshing around in her belly. She smiles, contented. Thinks she ought to be the poster girl for the Got Milk? ads.

10:59 p.m.

Janie pulls herself out of her post-dinner stupor and wonders what Cabel's doing in her room all this time. She gets up and heads down the short hallway, pushes the door open, and gets sucked into darkness immediately.

She staggers.

Drops to the floor.

Cabel's frantic, trying to lock a door. Each time he locks it, another lock appears. As he secures each new one, the others spring open. He can't keep up.

Janie reaches for the door, blindly.

Backs out of her room on her hands and knees, pulling the door shut with her.

And the connection is broken.

She blinks, seeing stars, and gets back to her feet. Pulls a ratty old blanket from the closet and settles on the couch, sighing. She can't even sleep in her own bed these days.

January 7, 2006, 6:54 a.m.

Janie is startled awake. She looks around as a cold blast of air washes over the living room. She sits up and goes to the kitchen, looking out the window. Fresh footprints in the snow lead down the drive, across the street, and into the yard on the other side.

She checks her bedroom.

He's gone.

She shakes her head. *What a jerk*, she thinks.

Then she finds his note.

J.,
Shit, I'm such a jerk. I'm sorry—you should
have smacked me awake. I've got some
things to do today, but will you call me?
Please?
Love,
Cabe

There's something about a guy who admits he's a jerk that makes him forgivable.

Janie climbs into her bed. Her pillow smells like him. She smiles. Hugs it.

Talks to herself.

"I would like to dream about Center Street and I

would like to talk to Miss Stubin again," she says over and over as she drifts off to sleep.

7:20 a.m.

Janie rolls over and rouses herself. Looks at the clock. Sighs. She's rusty at it. Repeats her mantra. Pictures the scene in her head.

8:04 a.m.

She's standing on Center Street. It's dark, cool, and rainy again.

Looks around.

No one is there.

Janie wanders up and down the street, looking for Miss Stubin, but the street is vacant. Janie sits on the bench where she sat before.

Waits.

Wonders.

Recalls the previous conversation.

"When you have questions about my notes, return here," Miss Stubin had said.

Janie slaps her hand to her forehead and the dream fades.

When Janie wakes, she vows to practice directing and controlling her dreams every night. It will help. She knows it will.

She also vows to keep reading Miss Stubin's notes, so she can come up with some questions.

10:36 a.m.

Janie munches on toast as she pulls out the box of files from Captain. She begins where she left off, and reads the reports, fascinated.

4:14 p.m.

She finishes the second file. Still sitting on her bed in her pajamas. Remains of snacks everywhere. The phone rings, and with a gasp she remembers Cabel's note from this morning. "Hello?"

"Hey."

"Shit."

He laughs. "Can I come over?"

"I'm totally still sitting here in my pajamas. Give me thirty minutes."

"You got it."

"Hey, Cabe?"

"Yes?"

"Why are you mad at me?"

He sighs. "I'm not mad at you. I promise. I just . . . I worry about you. Can we talk about this when I come over?"

"Sure."

"See you soon."

4:59 p.m.

Janie hears a light knock and the door opening. She peeks her head around the corner, and to her great surprise, it's Carrie.

"Hi, it's me, your fair-weather friend!" Carrie grins sheepishly.

Shit, Janie thinks.

She grabs her coat and puts on a smile. "Hey, girl," she says. "I was just going out to shovel. Care to join me?"

"Uh . . . I guess."

"What's up?"

"Nothin'. Just bored."

"Where's Stu?"

"Poker night."

"Ahhh. Does he do that regularly?"

"Not really. Just whenever the guys call him."

"Mmmm." Janie grabs the shovel and starts clearing the steps first, then the sidewalk. She keeps her face turned toward the direction she thinks Cabel will come from. It's growing dark, and she hopes he notices her.

"So, what are you doing tonight?"

"Me?" Janie laughs. "Homework, of course."

"You want company?" Carrie's looking wistful.

"Do you have homework to do?"

"Of course. Whether I do it or not is the real question."

Janie sees him out of the corner of her eye. He's stopped

still in the side yard of the neighbors across the street. She laughs with Carrie and says, "Well, that's enough of that." She bangs the shovel and climbs the steps. "Go on in," she says.

Carrie steps inside, and Janie gives Cabel a fleeting glance over her shoulder. He shrugs and flashes the okay sign. Janie follows Carrie in.

Carrie stays until midnight, when she's good and drunk on Janie's mother's liquor.

Janie thinks about going to Cabel's after Carrie leaves, but decides she'll get a good night's sleep here and see him in the morning.

January 8, 2006, 10:06 a.m.

Janie calls Cabel. Gets his voice mail.

11:22 a.m.

Cabel returns Janie's call. Leaves a message on the answering machine.

12:14 p.m.

Janie calls Cabel. Gets his voice mail.

2:42 p.m.

The phone rings.

"Hello?" Janie says.

"I miss you like hell," he says, laughing.

"Where are you?"

"At U of M. I had a thing to go to."

"Fuck."

"I know."

There is silence.

"When will you be home?"

"Late," he says. "I'm sorry, sweets."

"Okay," she says with a sigh. "See you tomorrow, maybe."

"Yeah. Okay," he says softly.

BIRTHDAY,
UNDERCOVER

January 9, 2006, 7:05 a.m.

Janie wakes up on her birthday feeling terribly sorry for herself.

She should know better.
This happens every year.
It seems worse this year, somehow.

She greets her mother in the kitchen. Her mother gives her a half-grunt, fixes her morning drink, and disappears into her bedroom. Just like any ordinary day.

Janie fixes frozen waffles for breakfast. Sticks a god-damn candle in them. Lights it. Blows it out.

Happy birthday to me, she thinks.

Back when her grandma was alive, she at least got a present.

She gets to school late. Bashful gives her a tardy, and won't reconsider.

Janie always hated Bashful.

Stupidest. Dwarf. Ever.

Psychology is interesting.

Not.

Mr. Wang is the most incompetent psych teacher in the history of the subject. So far, Janie knows more than he does. She's pretty sure he's just teaching until he makes his big break in showbiz. Apparently he likes to dance. Carrie told Janie that Melinda saw him in Lansing at a club, and he was tearing it up.

Funny, that. Because he seems very, very shy. Janie makes a note, and then spills her red POWERade over her notebook. It spatters on her shoe and soaks in.

And then, in chemistry, her beaker explodes.

Sends a shard of glass, like a throwing star, into her gut.

Rips her shirt.

She excuses herself from class to stop the bleeding. The school nurse tells her to be more careful. Janie rolls her eyes.

Back in class, Mr. Durbin asks if she'll stop by the room after school to discuss what went wrong.

Lunch is barfaritos.

Dopey, Dippy, and Dumbass are all on their toes today. Somebody falls asleep in each of those classes, even PE, because they're doing classroom studies on health today. Janie finally resorts to throwing paper clips at their heads to wake them up.

By the time she gets to study hall, she feels like crying. Carrie doesn't remember her birthday, as usual. And then, Janie realizes with that keen, womanly sense of dread that she has her period.

She gets a hall pass and spends most of the hour in the bathroom, just getting away from everybody. She doesn't have a tampon or a quarter to get one from the machine. So back to the school nurse for the second time that day.

The nurse is not very sympathetic.

Finally, with five minutes left of school, she heads back to the library. Cabel gives her a questioning look.

She shakes her head to say everything's cool.

He glances around. Slides into the seat across from her. "Are you okay?"

"Yeah, just having a shitty day."

"Can I see you tonight?"

"I guess."

"When can you come?"

She thinks. "I dunno. I've got some shit to take care of. Like five, maybe?"

"Feel like working out?"

Janie smiles. "Yeah."

"I'll wait for you."

The bell rings. Janie finishes up her English homework, gathers up her backpack and coat, and heads over to Mr. Durbin's room. She already knows why her beaker exploded, and she doesn't feel like telling him what happened.

She opens the door. Mr. Durbin's feet are propped up on the desk. His tie hangs loose around his neck, and the top button of his shirt is undone. His hair is standing up a bit, like he's run his fingers through it. He's grading papers on a clipboard in his lap. He looks up. "Hi, Janie. I'll be just a second here." He scribbles something.

She stands waiting, shifting her weight from one

foot to the other. She has cramps. And a headache.

Mr. Durbin scribbles a few more notes, then sets his pen down and looks at Janie. "So. Rough day?"

She grins, despite herself. "How can you tell?"

"Just a hunch," he says. He looks like he's trying to decide what to say next, and finally he says, "Why the cake and frosting?"

"I'm sorry?"

"Why did you put back the cake and frosting, out of all the other things you had in your cart?"

"I didn't have enough cash on me."

"I understand that. Hate when that happens. But why didn't you put back the grapes or carrots or something?"

Janie narrows her eyes. "Why?"

"Is it your birthday? Don't lie, because I checked your records."

Janie shrugs and looks away. "Who needs a cake, anyway," she says. Her voice is thin, and she fights off the tears.

He regards her thoughtfully. She can't read his expression. And then he changes the subject. "So. Tell me about your little explosion."

She cringes.

Sighs.

Points at the chalkboard.

"I'm having some trouble reading the board," she says.

Mr. Durbin taps his chin. "Well, that'll do it." He

smiles and slides his chair back. "Have you been to the eye doctor yet?"

She hesitates. "Not yet." She looks down.

"When's your appointment?" he asks pointedly. He stands up, gathers a beaker and the components for the formula, and sets them at her lab table. Waves her over.

"I don't have one yet."

"Do you need some financial help, Janie?" His voice is kind.

"No . . . ," she says. "I have some money." She blushes. She's not a charity case.

Mr. Durbin looks down at the formula. "Sorry, Janie. I'm just trying to help. You're a terrific student. I want you to be able to see."

She is silent.

"Shall we try this experiment again?" He pushes the beaker toward her.

Janie puts on her safety glasses, and lights the burner.

Squints at the instructions and measures carefully.

"That's one quarter, not one half," he says, pointing.

"Thanks," she mutters, concentrating.

She's not going to fuck this up again.

Mixes it up. Stirs evenly for two minutes.

Lets it come to a boil.

Times it perfectly.

Cuts the heat.

Waits.

It turns a glorious purple.

Smells like cough syrup.

It's perfect.

Mr. Durbin pats her on the shoulder. "Nicely done, Janie."

She grins. Takes off her safety glasses.

And his hand is still on her shoulder.

Caressing it now.

Janie's stomach churns. *Oh god*, she thinks. She wants to get away.

He's smiling proudly at her. His hand slides down her back just a little, so lightly she can hardly feel it, and then to the small of her back. She's uncomfortable.

"Happy birthday, Janie," he says in a low voice, too close to her ear.

Janie fights back a shudder. Tries to breathe normally. *Handle it, Hannagan*, she tells herself.

He steps away and begins to help her clean up the lab table.

Janie wants to run. Knows she needs to keep her cool, but instead she escapes at the first reasonable opportunity. It was one thing talking about what might happen, and it was an entirely different thing to actually experience it. Janie shudders and forces herself to walk calmly. Get her thoughts together.

She heads outside for the parking lot. And then she remembers she left her goddamned backpack on the goddamned lab table.

Her keys are in that bag.

The office is closed by now.

And she doesn't have a fucking cell phone. *Hi, this is 2006, calling to tell you you're a loser.*

She goes back anyway, feeling like a dork, and meets Mr. Durbin halfway. He's carrying it. "Thought I might find you on your way back for this," he says.

Janie thinks fast. Knows what she needs to do. She struggles to get over the creep factor. "Thanks, Mr. Durbin," she says. "You're the best." She gives his arm a quick squeeze, and flashes a coy smile. And then she turns and heads down the hallway, taking long, loose strides. She knows what he's looking at.

When she rounds the corner, she glances over her shoulder at him. He's standing there, watching her, arms folded across his chest. She waves and disappears.

And now she doesn't want to tell Cabel.

He's going to be upset.

She drives home and looks up Captain's number. Calls her cell phone.

Tells her about her hunch.

"Good job, Janie. You're a natural," she says. "You okay?"

"I think so."

"Can you keep it going for a while?"

"I—I'm pretty sure I can, yes."

"I know you can. Now I want you to research. Isn't there a chemistry fair or something? A high-school statewide competition that Fieldridge sends a team to? Something like that?"

"I don't know. Yeah, I think so. There must be. There's one for math, anyway."

"Check into it. If there is one, and this Durbin goes to it, I want you to sign up. We'll pay for it, don't worry about that. I've been racking my brain, and I can't think of any other way you're going to land in his or some of the other students' dreams. Can you?"

"No, sir. I mean, okay, I'll sign up." Janie sighs, remembering the bus trip to Stratford.

"Have you taken a look at Martha's reports yet?"

"Some," Janie says.

"Any questions?"

Janie hesitates, thinking about what Miss Stubin said in the dream. "Nope. Not yet."

"Good. Oh, and Janie?"

"Yes, sir?"

"You're calling from home. Haven't I given you a god-damned cell phone yet?"

"No, sir."

"Well, I don't want you to go anywhere without one from now on. You hear me? I'll have one for you tomorrow. Stop by after school. And you need to tell Cabel about this guy if you haven't already. I don't want you in this project alone. It already makes me ill, knowing that creep is hitting on other high-school girls, much less you."

"Yes, sir."

"One more thing," Captain says.

"Yes?"

There's a pause.

"Happy birthday. There's a gift on my desk for you. The cell phone will be next to it by tomorrow after school, if you come while I'm not here."

Janie can't speak.

She swallows.

"Is that clear?" Captain says.

Janie blinks her tears away. "Sir, yes, sir."

"Good." There's a smile in her voice.

It's well after six before Janie makes it to Cabel's house. She jiggles her keys, trying to find the right one, and he opens the door. She looks up at him. Smiles. "Hi."

"Where've you been?"

"Sorry. Stuff happened." She enters the house. Takes off her coat and boots.

"What stuff?"

She sniffs the air. "What are you cooking?"

"Chicken. What stuff?"

"Oh, you know. Got to school late, and everything fell apart after that. You ever have one of those days?"

He goes to the stove and flips the chicken. "Yeah. Practically every day last semester, when you wouldn't talk to me. So what happened?"

She sighs. "My beaker exploded. Third hour. Durbin. I had to go in after school to redo the experiment."

He looks at her, tongs in hand. "The guy with the groceries?"

She nods.

"And?"

"And . . . I think he's the guy we're after. I called Captain."

He sets the tongs down loudly on the counter. "What makes you think that?"

"He touched me. It was . . . weird." She says it quickly, and then turns and goes into the bathroom.

But he's right behind her, and she can't get the door closed because his foot is in the way. "Where?" he shouts.

She cringes. Squeaks. She takes a breath, gathers her nerve, and gives him a furious look. "Stop it, Cabe! If you can't handle this without getting in my face about it, I'm not going to tell you anything."

He hears her.

His eyes grow wide.

"Oh baby," he whispers. Steps back. Out of the doorway. His face is ashen. He walks slowly back to the kitchen. Leans over the counter. Puts his head in his hands. His hair falls over his fingers.

The bathroom door clicks shut.

She stays in there for a long time.

He's pulling his hair out.

Finally, frustrated, he calls Captain. "What's going on, sir?"

There is a pause, and then he says, "She said he touched her. That's all I've gotten out of her so far."

He nods.

Yanks his hair.

"Yes, sir."

He listens intently.

His face changes.

"It's what?"

Then.

"Bloody fucking fuck," he mutters. "You're kidding." He closes his eyes. "Shoot me now. I didn't know."

He turns off the phone.

Sets it on the table.

Walks to the bathroom door.

Leans his forehead against the molding.

"Janie," he says. "I'm sorry I yelled. I can't stand the thought of that creep touching you. I'll get a handle on it. I promise."

He waits. Listens.

"Janie," he says again.

Then gets worried.

"Janie, please let me know you're okay in there. I'm worried. Just say something, anything, so I—"

"I'm okay in here," she says.

"Will you come out?"

"Will you stop yelling at me?"

"Yes," he says. "I'm sorry."

"You're driving me crazy," she says, coming out. "And you scared me."

He nods.

"Don't do that."

"Okay."

7:45 p.m.

Cabel turns the burner on low under the chicken, hoping to salvage it. Janie's in the computer room, writing up her notes.

He comes in and sits opposite her, at the other computer. Does some surfing. Some typing. Hits Send. Janie's computer binks. When she finishes her notes, she checks her Gmail. Clicks on the link. Watches the screen.

It's a Flash e-card.

Simple and beautiful.

I love you, and I'm sorry I'm an asshole.
Happy birthday.
Love,
Cabe

She looks down at the keys. Composes her thoughts. Hits Reply.

Dear Cabe,
Thank you for the card.
It means a lot to me.
I haven't received a birthday card since I turned
nine. I just realized that was half my life ago.
I'm sorry I'm an asshole too. I know it frustrates
you when I don't take care of myself—that's why
you were mad the other day, isn't it? I'll try harder
to work on the dreams, so they don't mess me up so
badly. And I'll keep supplies in my backpack from
now on. I should have been doing that all along, so

you don't have to worry so much.

Thing is, I like it when you are there to help me. It
makes me feel like somebody cares, you know? So
maybe I've neglected some things on purpose, just so
you notice. It's stupid. I'll stop with that.

Why are you so upset about this case?

All I know is that I really miss you.

Love,

J.

She reads it over and hits Send.

Cabel's computer binks.

He reads the e-mail.

Hits Reply.

Dear J.,

I want to explain something.

After my dad set me on fire . . . Well . . . He died
in jail while I was still in the hospital getting skin
grafts. And I never got to tell him how much he hurt
me. Not just physically, but inside, you know? So I
took it out on other things for a while.

I'm better now. I got counseling for it, and I'm really
better. But I'm not perfect. And I'm still fighting it.

See . . . You're, like, the only person I have in my life
that I really care about. I'm selfish about that. I don't

want anybody to touch you. I want to keep you safe.
That's why I hate this assignment so much. Now that
I have you, I'm afraid to see you get hurt or messed
up, like I was. I'm afraid I'll lose you, I guess.
I wish you could always be safe. I worry a lot. If you
*weren't so damned independent . . . Ah, well. *smile**
As much as we have been through in the past few
months, we still don't know each other very well, do
we? I want to change that about us. Do you? I want
to know you better. Know what makes you happy and
what scares you. And I want you to know that about
me, too.
I love you.
I will try to never hurt you again.
I know I'll screw up. But I'll keep trying, as long as
you let me.
Love,
Cabe

Send.

Janie reads.

Swallows hard.

Turns toward him. "I want that too," she says. She stands up and scoots over onto his lap. Holds him around the neck. His arms circle her waist, and he closes his eyes.

January 10, 2006, 4:00 p.m.

Janie slips into the police station, goes through the metal detector, and heads downstairs.

"Hey, new girl," says a thirtysomething man when she gets to Captain Komisky's door and knocks. "Hannagan, right? Captain said to tell you to go on in. She left you some stuff. I'm Jason Baker. Worked with Cabel on the drug bust."

Janie smiles. "Pleased to meet you." She shakes his hand. "Thanks," she adds, and opens the office door. On the corner of the desk is the tiniest cell phone she's ever seen, and next to it is a medium-size box and an envelope. The box has a bow on it. She grins and takes the items, then slips back out. When she gets to the car, she examines the gift box and the envelope, savoring it.

Decides to wait.

4:35 p.m.

Sitting on her bed, she opens the envelope first. It's a traditional birthday card with a simple signature on the bottom—"Fran Komisky." Inside the card is a gift certificate to Mario's Martial Arts for a self-defense class. Cool.

And inside the box is every kind of pampering item that Janie would never buy for herself. Relaxation votives, stress massage oils, aromatherapy bath salts, and a plethora of scented lotions in tiny adorable bottles. Janie squeals. Best present ever.

She calls Mario's and signs up for a class that starts the next day. And then, she goes to the phone book and looks up optometrists. Finds a vision shop that's open evenings and calls for an appointment. The receptionist says there's a cancellation for a five thirty p.m. appointment today, and can she make it?

She can.

And does.

She raids her college fund.

Walks out an hour later, four hundred bucks poorer but wearing new, funky, sexy glasses. She loves them, actually.

And she can see.

She had no idea how poorly she was seeing before.

Can't believe the difference.

She drives straight to Cabel's, knowing she can't stay long. She knocks on the front door. He opens it, towel drying his hair. She grins brightly.

He stands there, gaping. "Holy shit," he says. "Get in here." He pulls her in the house and slams the door. "You look fantastic," he says.

"Thank you," she says. She bounces on the balls of her feet. "And an added bonus," she says.

"Let me guess. You can see?"

"How'd you know?"

"Just a hunch."

"Hey, let's trade!"

He grins slyly. Takes his off and hands them to her. She whips hers off and puts his on while he watches, amused.

"Holy Moses, your eyes are terrible."

"No," he says. "Yours are. My glasses are clear."

She takes his off and playfully pummels him in the chest. "You are *such* a dork! You don't even need to wear glasses?"

He clasps his hands around her back and holds her tight against him. "It was all part of the image," he says, laughing. "I kind of got used to them. I like the look, so I kept them. Makes me look sexy, don't you think?" he teases, and then kisses her on the top of the head.

"You smell great," Janie says. She wraps her arms around him and looks up. "Oh! Check this out." She reaches into her pocket and pulls out the cell phone. "I have no idea how it works, but isn't it the cutest little thing you've ever seen?"

Cabel takes the phone and examines it. Thoroughly. "This phone," he says finally. "I want this phone."

She laughs. "No. S'mine."

"Janie, I don't think you understand. I want it."

"Sorry."

"It's got photo Caller ID; Internet; video, camera, and digital recorder?! Holy Hannah . . . It's making me warm all over."

"Oh, yeah?" Janie says in a sexy voice. "Wanna play with my phone, baby?"

He looks at her, his eyes smoldering. "Hell yes, I do." He runs his fingers through her hair, slips his hands in the back pockets of her jeans, and leans down to kiss her.

Their glasses clink.

"Fuck," they whisper together, laughing.

"I can't stay, anyway," she says. "Plus, I'm parked in your driveway."

"Wait one second, 'kay?" Cabel slips away and comes back a moment later. "Here," he says, handing her a small box. "For you. For your birthday."

Janie's lips part in surprise. She takes it. Feels really strange about opening it in front of him. She wets her lips as she examines the box and the ribbon that surrounds it. "Thank you," she says softly.

"Um . . ." He clears his throat. "The gift, see, is actually inside the box. The box is like an extra bonus gift. It's how we do things here on planet Earth."

She smiles. "I'm still enjoying the box and the fact that you bought me a gift. You didn't have to do that, Cabe."

"I just wish you'd told me it was your birthday, so I could have had it on the right day."

"Yeah," she says with a sigh, "that was me, having a little pity party for myself. I should have said something. When's yours?" She says suddenly.

"November 25."

She looks up at him. Her eyes remember. "Thanksgiving weekend."

"Yeah. You were at the sleep study. And we weren't exactly on speaking terms."

"That must have been a shitty weekend," she says.

He's silent for a moment. "Open it, J."

She slides the ribbon off.

Opens the box. It's a tiny diamond pendant on a silvery chain. It sparkles in the box.

Janie gasps.

And bursts into tears.

THE GREEN
AND THE BLUES

January 26, 2006, 9:55 a.m.

Mr. Wang stops Janie after second hour. "Do you have a moment, Janie?"

"Sure," she says. Mr. Wang is dressed in Polo.

The room clears out.

"I just wanted to compliment you on your work so far. You seem to have a real understanding of psychology. Your essay answers on the first test were brilliant."

Janie grins. "Thanks."

"Have you ever thought of a career in psych?"

"Oh . . . you know. I've toyed with the idea a bit. I'm not sure yet what I'll go for in college."

"So you *do* have college plans?" His voice has a hint of incredulity to it. "Franklin Community, maybe?"

Janie blinks, feeling the snub.

Feeling poor.

As if living on the wrong side of town means less is expected of her.

"Well, I would," she says, her voice taking on an innocent twang, "if'n I didn't have Earl Junior on the way, and you know mamaw can't stay alone in the trailer so good no more. I got to go find Earl Senior, so I can git me some money, know whut I mean?"

Mr. Wang stares at her.

She turns away when the bell rings and walks in late to chemistry.

"Sorry," she mouths to Mr. Durbin as she slides into place at her lab table at the back of the room. The others are working already. Janie copies down the equations from the board. She is still amazed at how well she can now see.

She hunches over her desk and scratches the figures on a piece of notebook paper, working out the formula, checking and double-checking her work. Mr. Durbin strolls around the room, giving hints and joking occasionally with the students as usual. She joins in like the others.

Every now and then, she glances up to see where he is, watching his body language as he interacts with the students. He hasn't said or done anything inappropriate that Janie's seen since their little incident a few weeks before, and now Janie's starting to question her judgment. Did it really happen? Or was she feeling so badly about herself that day that she imagined it?

He really is a terrific teacher.

And then he's next to her at her table, checking out her work. "Looking good, Hannagan," he says quietly. But he's not looking at her formula, bubbling merrily over the burner.

He's looking down her shirt as she's leaning over.

After class he stops her on the way out the door. "Do you have a slip for me?"

Janie is stumped. "A what?"

"A note?"

"For what?"

"You were late."

Janie thumps her forehead. "Oh! Um . . . No, I don't, but Mr. Wang kept me after class last period. He'll vouch for me."

"Mr. Wang, hm?"

"Yes."

"Hang out here a moment while I call him."

"But . . ."

"I'll write you a note for your next class, don't worry." He picks up the phone and dials Mr. Wang's room.

Mr. Wang apparently confirms that he held Janie after class. The bell rings. Mr. Wang says something else, and Mr. Durbin chuckles. "Is that so." He listens again. "I'll say," he says. He gives Janie a sidelong glance. His eyes come to rest on her chest as he hangs up.

"Okay, you're off the hook," he says, smiling. "So, who's your baby daddy?"

She grins, embarrassed. "That was a little joke," she says, and wets her lips. "Thanks. Can you write me a note now?"

"Sure," he says lazily. He reaches for his pen and scribbles on a square sheet of recycled paper. He holds the note out in front of him, so she has to approach to get it. "How's that sound?" He's grinning.

She takes the paper. "You want me to read this?" she says.

He nods and scribbles on a second square of paper now. "And this is for your next teacher."

She reaches for it. "Oh, okay," she says. "Uh . . ."

"The first one is some information about a little chemistry party I have every semester at my house, just for the Chem. 2 students. Any chance you can whip up a flyer for me to hand out to everybody?"

Janie looks at the paper. "Of course, I'd love to."

"You look like the type who would be good with computer graphics," he says. "You know what I mean." He wiggles his fingers. "Savvy . . . with electronics."

"It must be my geeky glasses that gives me away," she says smoothly.

"The glasses are nice, Janie. Are they working out for you okay?"

"Yeah, great. Thanks for asking." She smiles. "I should . . . probably get to my next class now. Don't you have a class this period?"

"Nope. This is my free hour."

"Oh, cool. I've been meaning to ask you—Is there a chemistry fair or a competition that you take students to?"

Mr. Durbin taps his chin thoughtfully. "I wasn't planning to do it this year, because it's all the way up in the UP at Michigan Tech, but you're the third person to ask me about it. Are you interested in me getting a team together? We'd have to do it quickly. The fair's next month."

Janie's eyes light up. "Oh, yes," she says. "I'd love to go!"

"It's a heck of a drive all the way up there. We'd have to book a hotel. Is that . . . um . . . feasible? I don't think there are any scholarships available."

Janie smiles. "I could handle a couple hundred bucks, yeah."

Mr. Durbin eyes her. "I think it could be a great experience," he says, his voice low and slow.

She nods. "Well, cool! Let me know. And I'll get that flyer to you soon. You want ten copies?"

"No hurry. The party's not until the first week of March. Ten copies would be perfect. Actually, make it twelve, in case Finch loses his, like he loses everything else. Thanks, Janie."

"Anything for you," Janie says, and blushes. "I mean . . . you know." She laughs and shakes her head, like she's embarrassed. "Never mind."

He's smiling at her chest. "See you tomorrow."

2:05 p.m.

Janie sits at her table and sneaks her cell phone out of her backpack. She fires it up. Sends Cabel a text message to his phone. "Can you get Durbin's past Chem. 2 class lists?"

A few moments later she gets the reply. "Sure. CU@4?"

Janie leans forward and sees him. He winks. She smiles and nods.

3:15 p.m.

Janie calls Captain.

"I may have talked Durbin into taking a group to the chemistry fair. It's next month. Way the heck up in Houghton."

"Excellent job, Janie. He'll have to take a female chaperone with him. You should be perfectly safe."

"He's hosting a party for the Chem. 2 students too. I guess he does it every year in March and in November."

Captain pauses. Grabs her notes. "Bingo. Call number one was March 5. Call number two was early November. I think we've got something here, Janie. Good work."

Janie hangs up to a rush of nervous excitement. *This is too weird*, she thinks.

4:00 p.m.

At Cabel's house Janie recounts the conversation with Durbin from memory, even though she took notes once she got to her next class. Cabel refrains from getting upset, like he promised.

He has the previous semester's list, as well as the one from last spring.

"Smart thinking, Cabe."

"Tomorrow I'll track the girls from these previous classes to see what they're taking now."

"Great," she says.

Janie whips up a flyer for the Chem. 2 party. It's

set for Saturday night, March 4. She prints out fifteen copies. Hands two to Cabel. "One for you, one for Captain."

"You don't know how much I wish I could be there."

"You'll be nearby, won't you?"

"Hell yes."

She stands and gives Cabel a hug. "I've gotta go."

He looks at her longingly. "Should I be feeling badly about the fact that you haven't stayed overnight in three weeks?"

"How's tomorrow night sound?"

He smiles. "Saturday too?"

"Yeah. You don't have any 'things' to go to?"

"Not this weekend."

"It's a date."

"Sweet," he says. "See you." He pulls her toward him for a kiss, and then she's gone, sprinting across the snow.

6:37 p.m.

Janie tackles the Stubin files. She knows Captain wants her to get through them. And Janie's had them for nearly a month. But everything is so interesting, and she's learning like crazy. How to get information from a dream. How to know what to look for in one. Miss Stubin could occasionally pause and pan dreams, as if she were a camera, and see the things behind her as well as in front of her. A few times Miss Stubin mentioned rewinding to see something twice. Janie hasn't been able to do any of that yet. She's trying, every study hall. Maybe she'll try it with Cabel this weekend.

10:06 p.m.

Janie's nearing the end of the last file. She rubs her temples as she reads. Her head aches. She grabs an Excedrin and a glass of water from the kitchen, and returns to her reading.

She's fascinated. Enthralled. Building up a list of questions for Miss Stubin and planning a dream visit soon.

Finally she closes the last file and sets it aside. All that's left are a few stray papers and a thin, green spiral notebook.

Janie glances at the papers. They appear to be notes, scrawled in illegible handwriting that doesn't stay between the lines. All the other files were typed. Janie's glad she didn't have to try to read them all like this. They must have been written late in Miss Stubin's career, after she retired and lost her eyesight.

Janie sets the papers aside and opens the spiral notebook.

Reads the first line. It's written in a controlled, sprawling hand—it's infinitely more legible than the notes on the bed next to Janie. It looks like a book title.

A Journey Into the Light
by Martha Stubin

There is a dedication below the title.

This journal is dedicated to dream catchers. It's written expressly for those who follow in my footsteps once I am gone.

The information I have to share is made up of two things: delight and dread. If you do not want to know what waits for you, please close this journal now. Don't turn the page.

But if you have the stomach for it and the desire to fight against the worst of it, you may be better off knowing. Then again, it may haunt you for the rest of your life. Please consider this in all seriousness. What you are about to read contains much more dread than delight.

I'm sorry to say I can't make the decision for you. Nor can anyone else. You must do it alone. Please don't put the responsibility on others' shoulders. It will ruin them.

Whatever you decide, you are in for a long, hard ride. I bid you no regrets. Think about it. Have confidence in your decision, whatever you choose.

Good luck, friend.

Martha Stubin, Dream Catcher

Janie feels her stomach churning.

She slides the notebook off her lap.

Closes it.

Stares at the wall, barely able to breathe.

Buries her head in her hands.

And then.

Slowly.

She picks up the notebook.

Puts it in the box.

Stacks the files on top of it.

And hides it deep in her closet.

3:33 a.m.

Janie's falling at top speed. She looks down dizzily and Mr. Durbin is there, waiting for her to land. He's laughing evilly, arms outstretched to catch her.

Before he can grab her, Janie swoops sideways and is sucked into Center Street, pulled through the air to the park bench and deposited there. Mr. Durbin is gone.

Next to the bench, in her wheelchair, sits Martha Stubin.

"You have questions," Miss Stubin barks.

Janie tries to catch her breath, alarmed. She grips the bench's armrest. "What's going on?" she cries.

Miss Stubin's gaze is vacant. A blood tear drips from the corner of her eye and slides slowly down her wrinkled cheek.

But all she says is, "Let's talk about your assignment."

"But what about the green notebook?" Janie grows frantic.

"There is no green notebook."

"But . . . Miss Stubin!"

Miss Stubin turns her face toward Janie and cackles.

Janie looks at the woman.

And then.

Miss Stubin transforms into Mr. Durbin. Slowly his face melts until all that remains is a hollow skull.

Janie gasps.

She breaks out into a cold sweat.

And wakes up, sitting straight up in bed and screaming.

Janie whips off her blankets and hops to her feet, turns on her light, and paces between the door and the bed, trying to calm down.

"That wasn't real," Janie tries to convince herself. "That wasn't Miss Stubin. It was a nightmare. It was just a nightmare. I didn't try to go there."

But now she is afraid to go to sleep.

Afraid to go back to Center Street again.

January 27, 2006

Janie's mind is far away, inside the front cover of a green spiral notebook and dwelling on her nightmare. She walks down the school hallways in a daze, nearly bumping into Carrie between classes with Bashful and Doc.

"Hey, Janers, wanna hang out tonight?"

"Sure." Janie thinks. "Um, I mean, I can't. Sorry."

Carrie gives her an odd look. "You okay? You're not gonna keel over, are you?"

Janie shakes the cobwebs from her head and grins. "Sorry. No, I'm fine. I've just got my mind on other shit. Colleges and stuff. I've got a bunch of junk to fill out, the house is a mess, and I'm working on a nasty headache already today."

"Okay," Carrie says. "I just thought you might like the latest gossip." She looks crestfallen. Of course, lately, Carrie only wants to hang out with Janie if Stu is playing poker. Janie doesn't mind being called upon only when Carrie's first choice is busy, though. She keeps busy enough without Carrie hanging around all the time.

"What about Melinda?"

"Thanks," Carrie says sarcastically, "but you don't need to set up a playdate for me. I can find my own things to do. I'll catch you later."

Janie blinks. "Whatever," she says under her breath. And walks into Mr. Wang's room. He's watching her walk in as he pretends to look at a paper in his hands. She smiles automatically. When he doesn't smile or look away, she winks.

That does it.

He flushes and sits down abruptly.

Third hour. Mr. Durbin's class. Janie waits until after class to present the flyers for the March 4 party. She takes her time packing up her table. Soon she is the last one there. From the corner of her eye, she sees Mr. Durbin watching her.

She pulls the flyers out and hurries up to his desk, like she doesn't want to be late for her next class. "Does this look all right?"

He takes them and gives an approving whistle. "Great," he says. He turns to her and raises his eyebrows. "I like," he says, staring at her now.

She leans forward on his desk, just slightly. "There's more where that came from," she says. "If you ever need any."

He swallows. "I'll have to take you up on that sometime."

She smiles. "Gotta go."

"Before you go," Mr. Durbin says, "I've got the okay on the chem. fair and a team of seven students, if you're game. It's February 20. We'll leave Sunday the nineteenth at noon, set up our display, stay overnight, do the fair, and start home around six p.m. on Monday, so we only miss one day of class. Here's the info and permission slip for your parents to sign. Cost is two hundred and twenty bucks, plus money for meals. You in?"

Janie grins. "I'm in." She takes the slip of paper from Mr. Durbin and darts out the door before she's late to her next class, glancing as she runs at the list of students who will be on the Fieldridge team. Janie's the only one from her class who is going.

Excellent, she thinks.

Dopey, Dippy, and Dumbass are the same as always. Janie actually likes PE now, since Cabel got her into working out. Although she could do without Dumbass. She also adores her self-defense class she's taking twice a week. Sometimes Cabel lets her practice on him.

Not really very often, though.

Not after she landed his ass on the floor.

PE is coed again, and Dumbass Coach Crater likes to use her as an example for why they no longer play guys versus girls with contact sports. It's because she cracked Cabel's 'nads in a basketball game last semester. On purpose.

Today, Dumbass makes them do the state-required strength tests, and Janie takes the class record for the girls in the flexed-arm hang. Dumbass notices her muscular arms and shoulders, and calls her Buffy as she's hanging there. She rolls her eyes and wishes he'd stand right in front of her. If she ever sees him on a dark street, she'll teach him to sing, she decides.

Study hall is quiet. Janie only gets sucked into one dream, and it's a weak one. Not a nightmare. When she realizes it's a sex fantasy between two fellow seniors who she really doesn't want to see naked, she doesn't stick around. She pulls herself out of it.

Smiles triumphantly.

Cabel's watching her, and she gives him the thumbs up and flashes a smile. He grins back.

Janie finishes all her homework for the weekend, so she jots down a few notes about Durbin and Wang.

Correction: make that Happy and Doc.

And then she sits there. Staring into space.

Thinking about Miss Stubin and the green spiral notebook. Feeling a sense of . . . well . . . dread.

On the way home from school Janie makes a quick dash into the grocery store to pick up some things for her house, so her mother doesn't starve to death, and a few personal items for the weekend. She packs an overnight bag. Toothbrush, shampoo, and the massage oil and candles that she got from Captain. She shoves it all in her backpack and heads over to Cabel's, leaving her mother a note on where to find her if she needs anything.

They work out, shower, and then lounge side by side in the giant beanbag chair and talk about the day. But Janie's having trouble keeping her mind on topic. She grows quiet, thinking about the green notebook and the assignment from Captain.

Cabel notices.

"Where are you?" he says after a while.

Janie startles. Smiles at Cabel. "I'm sorry, sweets— I'm here." But she's not really there. She's going over the Durbin/Stubin dream in her head, now more convinced it was a nightmare and not really a visit from Miss Stubin.

Cabel sits up quietly. Watches her face. Clears his throat.

Janie sees him suddenly, the one guy she wants to be with—and is with for the whole weekend—hovering over her. She shakes the thoughts of creepy nightmare Durbin from her brain and tilts her head to the side, grinning. "Oops. I did it again."

Cabel gives her a quizzical look. "I am totally not getting enough attention here."

Janie thumbs his cheek. Pulls his face to hers and kisses him, her tongue darting across his teeth playfully until she coaxes him to play along.

A surge of something—love?—makes Janie's skin tingle. But it scares her, too, when she thinks of her future, always with this dream curse hanging over her. She never thought she'd be with someone. Never imagined someone would sacrifice so much to deal with her strange problems. Wonders when Cabel will get tired of it all and give up on her.

Desperately she pushes that thought aside. Her lips are hot against his neck.

She tugs at his T-shirt and slips her quivering fingers under it, re-exploring Cabel's nubbly skin. Touching the scars on his belly, his chest. She knows that Cabel feels the same way she does, sometimes—like no one would want to be with him because of his issues. *Maybe the two of us really could last*, Janie thinks. *Misfits, united.*

Cabel's fingers trace a slow path from Janie's shoulder to her hip as they kiss. Then he slips his shirt over his head and tosses it aside. Presses against her. "That's a little better," he whispers in her ear.

"Only a little?"

The winter dusk of late afternoon falls into the room. Janie reaches for her blouse and slowly unbuttons it. Lets it fall open.

Cabel pauses and stares, not sure what to do. He closes his eyes for a moment and swallows hard.

She reaches between her breasts and unhooks her bra.

And then she turns her face slowly toward him. "Cabel?" She looks into his eyes.

"Yes," he whispers. He can barely get the word out.

"I want you to touch me," she says, taking his hand and guiding it. "Okay?"

"Oh god."

She pulls a newly purchased condom from her pocket.

Sets the package on the skin of her belly.

Reaches for his jeans.

Cabel, momentarily rendered speechless, helpless, and thoughtless except for wanting her, sighs in shudders as he touches her skin, her breasts, her thighs, and then, as the light fades from the window, they are kissing as if their lives depend on their shared breath, and urgently making love for the first time, with their eyes and bodies, like it's the only chance they'll ever have.

In the evening, as they lie together in Cabel's bed, she knows it's time. Before she reads the green notebook, before what happens, happens, she needs to say what she feels. Because he is the only one who matters.

She practices in her mind.

Forms the words with her mouth.

Then tries them, softly, out loud.

"I love you, Cabe."

He's quiet, and she wonders if he's sleeping.

But then he buries his face in her neck.

February 1, 2006

Janie spends the school week swapping sexual innuendos with Mr. Durbin, trading confusing glances with Mr. Wang, and bantering spiteful barbs with Coach Crater.

Cabel tracks down the whereabouts of last semester's Chem. 2 class. He's working madly behind the scenes, not saying much about it. Controlling his feelings about the creep being near the woman he loves. Knowing if he says what he's really thinking, the tension grows between them.

"So," he says carefully, "it's you and six other students on this trip, plus Durbin. And who's your female chaperone?"

Janie glances up from her chemistry book. "Mrs. Pancake."

Cabel scribbles in his notebook.

"Four girls. You have a room together?"

"No, I thought I'd sleep in Durbin's room," Janie says.

"Har, har." Cabel scowls at Janie, and then tosses her chemistry book aside and tackles her. He buries his fingers into her hair and kisses her. "You're asking for trouble, Hannagan," he growls.

"And you would be . . . ?" Janie asks. She giggles.

"Trouble."

ON HER OWN

February 5, 2006, 5:15 a.m.

Janie, sprawled out on Cabel's couch, finally finds Miss Stubin on Janie's own terms.

She's on the bench. Miss Stubin is there, next to her. It's dusk. Perpetual rain.

"I'm going on an overnight trip with the teacher who we think is the sexual predator. Some of his former students are going too—they may be victims," Janie says.

"What season is it?" Miss Stubin asks.

Janie looks at her, puzzled. "Winter. It's February."

"Wear a bulky coat to disguise the shaking in case you

get sucked into a nightmare. Drape it over you. You're taking a school van?"

"Yes."

"Grab the backseat. And if you get sucked into a dream that's unimportant to the case, pull out of it. Don't waste your strength. You can pull out of them now, can't you?"

"Most of the time—the regular dreams, anyway. Not always with nightmares."

"Keep working at that. It's very important."

"I want to try pausing the dreams. Panning the scene. How did you do that?"

"It's all about focus, just as you focus to pull out of dreams, Janie. Just as you focus to help people change their dreams. Stare hard at the subject and talk to them with your mind. Tell them to stop. Focus on panning first—that comes most easily. Then pausing the scene. Who knows, perhaps you'll be able to zoom and rewind someday—that really comes in handy when solving crimes. And keep studying the meanings of dreams too. You've read books on the subject, haven't you?"

"Yes."

"Your work will be easier the more you can interpret some of the strange aspects that naturally occur in dreams. This, too, will help you immensely. Study my notes, see how I've interpreted dreams over the years."

Janie nods, then blushes, remembering Miss Stubin can't see her. "I will. Miss Stubin?"

"Yes, Janie?"

"About the green notebook . . ."

"Ah, you've found it, then."

"Yes."

"Go on."

"Does Captain know about it? About what's in it?"

"No. Not the notebook."

"Does she know anything about how dream catching works?"

"Some," Miss Stubin says guardedly. "We talked a little over the years. She's certainly someone you can talk to when you need to."

"Does anyone else understand this besides you and me?"

Miss Stubin hesitates. "Not that I know of."

Janie fidgets. "Should I read it? Do you want me to? Is it horrible?"

Miss Stubin is silent for a very long time. "I can't answer those questions for you. In good conscience, I can neither encourage you to read it nor discourage you from reading it. You must decide without my words swaying you either way."

Janie sighs and reaches for the old woman's hand, stroking the cool, paper-thin skin. "That's what I thought you'd say."

Miss Stubin pats her gnarled hand on top of Janie's soft one. She smiles wistfully and slowly disappears into the misty evening.

7:54 a.m.

It's Sunday morning. And it's time. It's been ten days since Janie found the green spiral notebook.

She slips back into bed with Cabel for a few minutes. He's just dozing now, not dreaming, and she holds him tightly, taking in whatever she can from him before she goes.

"I love you, Cabe," she whispers.

And goes.

Back to her room two streets away.

8:15 a.m.

With the notebook resting ominously on Janie's bed, Janie procrastinates.

Does her homework first.

And pours herself a bowl of cereal. Breakfast—one of the five most important meals of the day. Not to be skipped.

10:01 a.m.

She can't stall any longer.

Janie stares at the green notebook.

Opens it.

Reads the first page again.

Takes a deep breath.

10:02 a.m.

Takes another deep breath.

10:06 a.m.

Picks up her cell phone and hits memory #2.

"Komisky," she hears.

Janie's voice squeaks. She clears her throat. "Hi, Captain. I'm sorry to call on a—"

"It's okay. What's up?"

"Um, yeah. The dreams . . . Did Miss Stubin ever show you what was in the files?"

"I've read the police reports she's made, yes."

"What about her other notes on handling dreams and stuff?"

"I glanced at the first few loose pages in the file, but I felt like I was invading her privacy, so I put everything away as she requested."

"Did you two ever . . . you know, talk about her ability?"

There is silence.

Plenty of it.

"What do you mean?"

Janie cringes silently. "I don't know. Nothing."

Captain hesitates. "All right."

"Okay."

There is a nervous sigh.

"Captain?"

"Janie, is everything okay?"

Janie pauses.

"Yeah."

Captain is quiet.

Janie waits. And Captain doesn't press it.

"Okay," Janie says finally.

"Janie?"

"Yes, sir." It's a whisper.

"Are you worried about Durbin? Do you want out of this?"

"No, sir. Not at all."

"If something else is bothering you, you may say it, you know."

"I know. I'm . . . I'm fine. Thanks."

"May I give you some advice, Janie?"

"Sure," Janie says.

"It's your senior year. You're too serious. Try to have some fun. Go bowling or to a movie or something once in a while, okay?"

Janie grins shakily. "Yes, sir."

"Call me anytime, Janie," Captain says.

Janie's throat is closed. "Bye," she finally says.

Hangs up.

10:59 a.m.

Janie takes a deep breath.

Turns the page.

It's blank.

11:01 a.m.

Turns the blank page.

Sees the familiar scrawl.

Smoothes out the page.

And then her stomach lurches, and she slams the notebook shut.

Puts it back in the box.

Into the closet.

11:59 a.m.

Janie calls Carrie. "Do you feel like going bowling?"

She imagines Carrie shaking her head and laughing, telling Stu, coming back to the phone. "You are such a dork, Hannagan. Hell yeah, why not. Let's go bowling."

NITTY GRITTY

February 13, 2006

The names and schedules of Chem. 2 students are burned in Janie's brain. But the problem is, most science nerds don't sleep in school. And even if they did, the issue remains of how Janie can be in the same room with them when—if—it happens. It appears impossible.

And seeing how it's winter, it's futile to creep around outside their bedroom windows at night. She has high hopes for the chemistry fair. It's all she has to bank on.

Cabel tries making a connection with each student on the list. He has more of them in his classes than Janie does. But they remain aloof, associating him with the popular Hill crowd, because of his past ties to Shay Wilder. He's frustrated.

There are eighteen Chem. 2 students in all this year. There were thirteen Chem. 2 students last year. All thirteen graduated and went to college, Cabel discovers, some of them as far away as southern California. Doggedly, Cabel tracks them, in case their lives changed somehow in the nine months since graduation. He spends hours each evening on the computer, checking their blogs, their Facebook and Myspace pages, looking for any wild tales they may have thought they were keeping semiprivate.

And together, they have a whole lot of nothing.

The one and only lead Janie has at the moment is Stacey O'Grady from first semester of Chem. 2. She's in Janie's study hall. Stacey has horrible nightmares, if she sleeps at all. Which is rare.

But lots of people have horrible dreams, and it doesn't mean anything, as far as Janie can tell. Even if the dream is about a rapist. Janie knows that a dream about being chased by a rapist could possibly be literal, but more likely it's a hint of an underlying fear in some other part of your life. The fear that something's catching up to you, or that you can't run fast enough, or that you've lost your voice and can't scream—all could simply indicate being overwhelmed with school or home pressures or feeling helpless to change things. Being a senior could do that to many people.

Still, Janie wills Stacey to fall asleep in study hall again, so she can get a better look.

Six of the ten students in Janie's Chem. 2 class are female. She doesn't know any of them well, although they're friendly enough with one another. None of them are going to the chem fair.

When Desiree Jackson suggests a study group night at her house before an upcoming test, Janie jumps at it. Maybe she can get some information that way. Several others like the study group idea too. They agree to meet Thursday night at seven at Desiree's.

Mr. Durbin hands out the flyers for the March 4 party, and Janie raises a question. "What do you think about inviting the first semester group to join us? More people, more fun, I'm thinking. Or maybe you don't have room for so many in your house, Mr. Durbin."

Janie has driven by Mr. Durbin's house. Cabel managed to snag the floor plan from the township office. She's got it memorized. It's a three-bedroom home with a large kitchen that overlooks the spacious great room. With its finished basement, the house is easily large enough for twenty or more.

Mr. Durbin scratches his chin. "I like that idea. Class, what do you think? You guys good with that?"

The class wants to know who those people would be. Mr. Durbin flips through the eight names by memory, and the consensus is affirmative.

"Cool," Janie says. "I'll make some more flyers. We should get a head count on how many are planning on coming."

"Good idea. Sheesh, eighteen kids. You guys are gonna break my bank account," Mr. Durbin jokes.

Several girls offer to bring appetizers, and Mr. Durbin gratefully accepts the offer. Janie's puzzled now. She thought he might balk at the idea. But he's giving no indication of this being anything other than a cool party for science geeks.

"Don't let me see you bringing any alcohol," Mr. Durbin says lightly, and grins like he's young enough to be hip with the thoughts of seniors and wants to nip it in the bud. But the mere acknowledgment sets several students exchanging mischievous glances.

He said that on purpose, Janie thinks. *To get the students thinking about it.*

After class Mr. Durbin stops Janie. "Good idea for the party, Janie. Maybe a few of you girls could come early to help set it up?" He's giving her a helpless bachelor look.

The back of Janie's neck is prickling, but she smiles

excitedly. "Awesome. This is going to be a blast! You are such a cool teacher. You're just like one of us, you know?"

Mr. Durbin grins. "I try. It's only been eight years since I was a senior in high school. I'm not some old geezer, you know." He's languid, leaning against the side of his desk, arms crossed in front of him.

And then he's reaching out his hand. "Hold still," he says. "You've got an eyelash." He brushes lightly across Janie's cheek with his thumb, and his fingers linger at her hairline just a second longer than necessary.

Janie lowers her eyes demurely, then looks back up into his. "Thanks," she says softly.

He gives her a smoldering look that is unmistakable. Janie hesitates a moment, then waves her fingers lightly as she turns and hurries out the door to her next class.

In study hall, Janie finds Stacey and slides into the chair across from her. Janie wants to be the first to announce the invitation to the party at Mr. Durbin's, so she can gauge Stacey's reaction. "Hi," she says with a grin.

Stacey looks up from her book with surprise. "Oh, hey, Janie. What's up?" Janie notes with a creepy shudder that she's reading Margaret Atwood's *The Handmaid's Tale*.

"You were in Durbin's Chem. 2 class last term, right?"

"Yesss . . ." Stacey looks suspicious.

"And you're going to the chemistry fair, right?"

"Oh, that. Yeah—you are too?"

"Yep. Sounds like fun. I'll be at the meeting next week to create our display."

"Cool. It should be easy enough."

"Anyway, I'm actually here to ask you about Durbin."

Stacey's eyes narrow. "What about him?"

"Well, he's having his Chem. 2 party at his house, and our class decided to invite your class to come too."

Stacey gets a goofy smile on her lips. "Oh cool! He didn't, by chance, tell you guys what happened last semester, did he?"

Janie cocks her head. "No, not really. Just said everybody had a great time."

Stacey's grin grows wider. She leans forward across the table, and whispers, "Everybody got completely plastered. Even Durbin and Wang."

Janie's heart jumps. She controls her surprise, and speaks softly. "Wang was there too?"

"Yeah. Durbin and Wang are buddies. I think they play a lot of rec basketball together or something. Durbin said something about Wang being there for entertainment and crowd control." She laughs, and then grows serious. "Don't tell anybody about the alcohol, 'kay? Durbin and Wang could both get canned for it. But we chem geeks are a loyal bunch. And we know how to keep our mouths closed," she adds. She's chuckling to herself.

"Of course," Janie says seriously. "I'd never rat on him—He's the best."

"Yeah." Stacey sighs. "He's sooo hot. Wang's not bad either, for a snooty guy who lives up on the Hill." The girls giggle softly, and Janie pulls out an extra copy of the party flyer. "Here's the info. Do you think you can make it? We're getting a head count so we know how much food to make."

"Hell yes, I'll be there. I could use a break from this crazy pace. You want me to spread the word? Most of the others are in my physics class."

"Sure. I'll get you some more flyers tomorrow."

"Sweet. And that was real cool of your class to invite us," she adds with a grin.

Janie grins back. "So, you think most of them will want to be there?"

Stacey thinks a moment. "I can't think of anyone who wouldn't jump at the chance."

7:02 p.m.

Janie wraps up her notes at Cabel's house, and muses, "This is getting curiouser and curiouser."

Cabel reads over her shoulder. He growls lightly. "He did that lame eyelash trick on you? God, what a loser." He begins pacing.

"Easy, big fella," murmurs Janie distractedly as she types in the info she got from Stacey that day. When she finishes, she flips screens to the party flyer and prints out ten copies.

Cabel's on the phone.

"It's Cabe," he says. "I think we need to watch Durbin's house in the evenings up until—" He pauses. "Oh. Well, that's why you're in charge." He grins sheepishly into the phone. "Thank you, sir."

He hangs up. "Did you know Captain's been surveilling Durbin's house for two weeks already?"

"Nope. But it's a good idea. How's your progress going, Cabe? I think it's strange that I can't find a single student who doesn't like Durbin. Have you been able to approach that question yet with your new contacts?"

"Some. He seems to be gunning for teacher of the year, though, the way things are going."

"If a student was the one who made the call, what would make them *not* follow through and get their reward? I don't understand that. Not everybody drinks. And if they showed up there last year not knowing it was that kind of a party, wouldn't they back out slowly, or at least talk to somebody about it? I've never heard of this happening before. You'd think Carrie'd know."

Cabe begins pacing again. After a while he says, "Carrie wouldn't know. She and Melinda and Shay and people into high-end Hill parties aren't science geeks. There's not one person on the list who I've ever seen at a Hill party. It's two different worlds."

"So, what is Durbin's hold over the geeks that makes them want to protect him?"

Cabel's in the zone. Janie can almost see the wheels turning in his head. She glances at the flyers, and on a whim, goes to her Gmail account and types up an e-mail to the address Mr. Durbin gave her.

Hey Mr. Durbin,

I talked to Stacey O'Grady today, and she's stoked about being invited to your party. She told me you guys had a terrific party last semester. If it's okay with you, she's going to distribute the flyers to the other kids from that class. Would it be cool if she and I came about an hour early to help you set it up?

And I know you said no alcohol, but I've got this great dessert recipe I wanted to bring . . . It has crème de menthe in it. Just a little. Not enough to get anybody even a buzz from eating a huge piece. Would that be okay with you? If not, I could always bring Rice Krispies treats instead.

Janie Hannagan

P.S. I'm a little worried about Friday's big test—trying to study and get ready for the chem fair is taking up a lot of time. Can I set up a meeting to talk over some formulas with you?

Thanks. J.

She presses Send and keeps the computer booted, turning up the volume a notch, just in case he's online and gets back to her quickly.

"What are you doing?" Cabel says suddenly.

"Flirting with Durbin."

"Oh." He turns back to his pacing, and then stops again. "You know, I think I finally understand how it felt for you. Remember when you stopped by my house and Shay was over?"

"Ah . . . yeah. It's burned like a cross into my brain."

"I didn't want you to see that. Not because I wanted to hide it from you. But because it would hurt."

Janie smiles at him. "I know. Sucks, doesn't it."

"It's driving me nuts," Cabel admits. "If that bastard hurts you, I'll kill him. I'm still not sure about you putting yourself in a position like that."

"Good thing I don't work for you, then." She knows it's harsh.

He stops pacing. Looks at her. "Damn. You're right." Starts pacing again. "So, do you think Durbin is hot?"

"I can see why girls are attracted to him."

"Are you attracted to him?"

Janie sighs. "Oh Cabe. Shay is hot, rich, sexy, popular. A cheerleader. Were you attracted to her?"

"No. She was a facet of my job."

"Exactly."

"You didn't answer my question."

Janie hesitates, wanting to be truthful. "Durbin is attractive. I can't deny that. But when he did the eyelash thing, it made the hair stand up on the back of my neck. He creeps me out, Cabe."

Cabel nods absentmindedly as he walks. "Okay. That makes me feel better."

She smiles. Gets it—it was the same with Cabel and Shay. And is proud of him for the new way he's approaching it now. "I love you, you know," she says. It's getting easier to say.

He comes over to where she's sitting and massages her shoulders lightly. But his voice is grim. "I love you too, Janie."

"And I'm getting really good at protecting myself," she adds. "My self-defense class kicks ass."

He tugs her hair. "I'm glad you're taking that class. You're really getting buff, you know that? It's very sexy. As long as you're not beating me up."

"Don't make me hurt you," she murmurs. "Hey, can I stay tonight?"

"Wow, I don't know, jeez, I'm, like, really busy and shit. . . ."

She grins.

And then she hears the binking sound of an e-mail arriving.

Janie,

LOL! Bring the dessert. And the bottle.

And a resounding yes to everything else you asked me, and more.

I could do tomorrow (Tues.) after school, for us to go over the formulas in question. The rest of my afternoons are tied up until around 7 p.m., but if you don't need much equipment, you could always stop by my house after 7 either tomorrow or Wednesday.

Dave Durbin

"He is so freaking smooth," remarks Cabel. "He knows tomorrow is Valentine's Day, and there's not only a big basketball game, but also the pep rally after school and the Valentine's dance from seven to ten. He's not expecting you to make it then." Cabel thinks for a moment. "When you write him back, call him Dave. He's begging for it."

With that, Cabel walks away.

Janie purses her lips, and hits Reply.

Dave,

How's Wednesday around 8? I know right where you live. Thanks!

J.

She hits Send, and waits less than a minute before she has a reply.

> *Looking forward to it.*
> *Dave*

Janie shuts down the computer and finds Cabel in the living room, watching some old western on the movie channel. She slides in next to him.

"I'm going to his house Wednesday at eight," she says. "Will you spot me?"

He snakes his arm around her neck and tugs gently. "Of course," he says. "I'm going to alert Captain to it, too."

"'Kay," Janie says, snuggling close.

After a while of watching TV, the volume on too low to actually hear the story line, Cabe says, "I wish we could go out tomorrow night. I'm so tired of this routine, hiding out all the time. Our biggest excitement is lifting weights or deciding between green beans and broccoli."

Janie sighs. "Me too. Do you think we'll ever be able to go out on a date?"

"Yeah. Maybe this summer. For sure in the fall. Once we rid ourselves of the web of lies we leave behind at Fieldridge High."

It's a sober moment.

Janie nods.

Rests her head on his shoulder.

He tousles her hair.

"Hey Cabe?" she asks as they climb into bed.

"Yeah, baby?"

"Do you mind if I practice on your dreams tonight?"

"Of course not. You don't have to ask me."

"I feel weird about not asking you if I'm planning it in advance," she says.

"It's cool. You working on something in particular?"

"Yeah . . . I'm trying to TiVo."

He laughs. "What, you mean pause, rewind—that sort of thing?"

"Exactly."

"That'll be interesting. I hope you pull it off. You don't want to take me with you, do you?"

"Not this time. I need all the concentration I can muster. Once I get it, I'll gladly show you, though."

He turns off the light and lets his arm rest around her midsection. He strokes her belly with his thumb, like he's strumming guitar. "You know," he says, "you could really have fun with a good dream once you learn how to do that."

"Guess why I want to practice on you," she says with a smile in the darkness.

"Be careful or you might go to school tomorrow flushed with sex."

She chuckles softly. "All part of the plan, babycakes."

"Well, that oughta turn Durbin on." Cabel's voice turns bitter.

Janie turns toward Cabel. "Have you figured out yet why nobody narcs on Durbin?"

"I think so," Cabel says. "It's because he's only a few years older and good-looking and athletic, and he really acts as if he likes the science-type kids. He accepts their geek minds and praises them for it. He's the epitome of a cool, popular kid, whose groupies have never been popular in their lives. They lap it up."

Janie clears her throat.

Waits.

Clears it again.

"I—I mean," stutters Cabel, "ah, I mean, some of them are like that, and some, you know, some others, like you, for example, see right through the facade and . . . uh . . . shit like that."

"Mmm hmm," Janie says.

"And . . . I love you so much? And now I'm going to shut up and go to sleep, so you can manipulate my mind in a dozen ways and more?"

"Weak," she says. "But it'll do."

Cabel dreams.

Janie slides into the darkness, and then into the computer room.

It's a dream that's loosely based on the night they made love there. She's watching him, she's watching herself, curiously, surprised to see how quickly they find their rhythm together for the first time.

She concentrates with all her might. Stares at Cabel. *Pause*, she thinks, over and over again.

A minute goes by, but nothing changes.

Another minute.

And then the scene slows.

Ten seconds later it's paused. In a very interesting spot, Janie notes.

Janie looks around the room, trying to notice everything. The office items on the desk; the clock on the wall stopped as well; the color of everything. It's incredibly difficult to hold the scene there. And then she begins to lose it. She can feel her body shaking, weakening, and the dream slips into regular speed again.

Her head pounds. Her fingers are numb. She bumps Cabel with her behind, trying to wake him just enough so she doesn't have to use her waning energy to pull out of the dream too. She knows she can't do it after that. She can barely feel her arms and legs as it is, already.

Cabel takes in a sharp breath, and she can feel him against her backside, aroused in his sleep. He begins to stroke her numbing body while he's still in the dream. She can feel his touch, fading in and out on her skin, as she's seeing it in his mind. And she's stuck. And falling. And very aroused and blind and numb and watching it in her mind while feeling it on her body, all at the same time, and she wants it. Wants to make love right now. But she is completely paralyzed.

She can't move.
She can't feel anything.
She can't speak.

It can't happen. Not like this.
She needs to wake him up, before something happens. So they can do it right.

She takes all her strength, all her concentration, all her will. She bites blindly. Feels hair in her teeth. Pulls back with her neck.

And everything goes black.

She's shuddering.
Shaking.
Trying to catch a breath as she aches to see something. Anything. His face. She wants to see his face.

He's talking to her.

His hand is on her cheek, sliding through tears.

And she realizes it now.

Realizes that there will scarcely be a time when they roll together, unawares, and make love sleepily in the dead of a winter night, lingering on their dreams.

She's broken.

Her muscles are like water.

And he's there, lifting her shoulders, holding a glass to her lips, telling her to drink and swallow.

She can feel his fingers pushing the hair out of her eyes. Hear his voice in her ear. Smell his skin nearby. Taste the milk on her tongue, in her throat. And then slowly she sees shadows. Black and white, at first, and then his face, looking wild. His hair, flipping every which way. His cheeks flushed.

And she speaks roughly. "It's okay," she says.

But it's not okay.

Because she wants him, and now he's afraid to touch her like that.

He makes her eat.

Sits by the bed.

Waits for her sleep to come.

She finds him, awake, on the couch in the morning.

Sits in the crook of his body.

And they look at each other, both so very sorry and neither one needing to be.

Cabel, feeling helpless. Janie, trapped by her own ability. Despairing in their own minds for a while, until they can come to terms with the life that lies ahead. And each, in their private thoughts on this Valentine's Day, wonders briefly if it should go on.

If they should go on.

Torturing each other unexpectedly, indefinitely.

"Cabe," she says.

"Yes?"

"You know what always makes me feel better?"

He thinks a moment. "Milk?"

"Besides milk."

"What?"

"When you hold me. Tightly. Squeeze my body like you can't let go. Or lie on top of me."

He's quiet. "Serious?"

"I wouldn't joke about that. There's something about the pressure on my body that helps the numbness go away." She waits. Hopes she doesn't have to ask him point-blank.

She doesn't.

DURBIN DAZE

February 15, 2006, 8:04 p.m.

Janie pulls into Mr. Durbin's driveway.

Cabel's parked half a block away with a pair of binoculars and a view through the side window of the great room.

Baker and Cobb are stationed.

Janie's not wired.

No one expects anything to happen.

Not quite yet.

Mr. Durbin's too smart to ruin it.

She grabs her books and walks to the front door. Rings the bell.

He opens the door. Not too quickly. Not slowly, either. Invites her inside.

She takes off her coat and hands it to him. She's wearing jeans and a low-cut, see-through shirt with a camisole underneath—an ensemble that wouldn't be allowed in school.

He's wearing sweatpants and a U of M T-shirt.

Sweating.

"Just got done working out," he says, draping a towel around his shoulders. He shows her to the kitchen table.

"Great house," she says. "Perfect for a party."

"Which is why I bought it," he says. "I like having a place for the students to kick back and crash now and then." He grabs a bottle of water, offers her one, and says, "You get organized. I'm going to take a three-minute shower. Be right back."

Janie rolls her eyes as he walks out, and then suddenly realizes.

He's gone.

She glides through the main floor, checking things out. She hears the shower running.

Two bedrooms and a bath down the hallway off the great room. An office beyond the kitchen area, with all sorts of science-type chemical charts and books and bottles. And a master suite, which is where he's showering. She peeks in quickly. It's a large room with a king-size bed and a few items of clothing strewn around. On the bedside table, a porn magazine.

She moves quickly back to the kitchen table when she hears the water shut off, and she's sitting there, looking engrossed in her notes, when he returns. Now he's wearing jeans and a white T-shirt, à la James Dean. All he needs is a cigarette.

He moves through the great room, closing blinds. Janie cringes internally, knowing that Cabel must be bristling right now. But Cabe promised Captain he'd be under control, and he knows he's not allowed to be on the case if he's not this way—he's too close to it. Janie thinks he'll stay put.

"Okay, kid, what seems to be the problem?" Durbin asks as he walks back toward the table. He sits in the chair next to her, running his fingers through his wet hair.

"Kid?" She laughs. "I'm eighteen."

"S'cuse me. What was I thinking. Ahhh," he says, leaning in to see her notes. "Poisonous gases." He rubs his hands together gleefully. "How exciting, eh?"

She turns and gives him a look. "Well, it's interesting. But I don't understand how this"—she points with her pencil—"leads to this. It doesn't make sense."

"Hrm," he says, and draws the pencil from her fingers slowly. "Let's start from the beginning."

He flips the paper over and scribbles equations expertly on the back side. Whistles lightly under his breath as he goes. Janie leans in, as if to see better, an inch at a time, until he's slowing his pencil.

Making a mistake or two.

Erasing.

Shifting in his seat.

She stops moving, and she's nodding slightly. Fully, completely, overwhelmingly enthralled by the scratching of his pencil.

She takes a sip of water from the bottle he offered, and her swallow is the only sound in the room.

She watches his Adam's apple bob reflexively.

"Okay," he says finally. He explains the half-page-long equation from start to finish, and she's turned toward him, her elbow on the table and fingers in her hair, nodding, thinking, waiting.

"I think I've got it," she says when he's finished.

"Now, you give it a try," he says, looking at her. He takes the paper and slips it under her notebook, brushing her breast with his forearm. Both pretend not to notice.

Janie pulls out a fresh piece of paper and begins from the initial equation. She leans over the paper, so her hair falls in front of her shoulder, and scribbles away. After a moment he draws her hair back over her shoulder. His fingers linger an extra moment on her neck. "I can't see," he explains.

"Sorry about that." She flips her hair to the other side of her neck, and she can feel him looking at her. She hesitates in the middle of the process. Mulls it over. "Hang on," she murmurs, "don't tell me."

"It's okay," he says quietly. He's leaning over her, his breath on her shoulder. "Take your time."

"I'm never going to get this," she says.

His fingers touch her back lightly.

She pretends not to notice.

She calculates her moves, trying to get into the mind of someone who would welcome such advances. She decides that the someone would do absolutely nothing now, not wanting to risk a problem, and so she lets out a shallow breath and moves her pencil again, and then after a moment, dares a quick glance at him that tells him everything he wants to know.

"How's that?" she asks, pointing to her work.

"It's good, Janie. Perfect." He lets his hand rest centrally on her back.

She smiles and looks at the paper a moment, and packs up her books slowly. "Well. Thanks, Mr. Durbin, for, uh, you know. Letting me barge in on your evening like this."

He walks her to the door and leans against it, his hand on the handle. "My pleasure," he says. "I hope you come by again sometime. Just shoot me an e-mail. I'll make it work."

She steps toward him, goes to open the door so she can leave, but he's still holding on to the door handle. Trapping her. "Janie," he says.

She turns. "Yes?"

"We both know, don't we," he says, "why you wanted to come here this evening."

Janie gulps. "We do?"

"Yes. And don't feel badly about it. Because I'm attracted to you, too."

Janie blinks. Blushes.

"But," he continues, "I can't have a relationship with you while you're my student. It's not right. Even though you're eighteen."

Janie is silent, looking at the floor.

He tips her chin up. His fingers linger on her face. "But once you graduate," he says with a look in his eye, "well, that's a different story."

She can't believe this.

And then she can.

It's how he keeps them quiet.

Blames them.

She knows what to say.

It's the *saying it* that makes her want to puke on his shoes.

"I'm sorry," she says. "I'm so embarrassed."

"Don't be," he says, and she knows he wants her to be.

She waits for it. Waits for the line she knows is coming next from this egocentric bastard. She resists the urge to say it first.

"It happens all the time," he says.

She manages to turn her cringe into a sad smile, and

leaves without another word, although she's tempted to follow the movie ending by crying out, "I'm such a fool!"

About four seconds after she pulls out of the driveway, her cell phone rings. She waits until she's out of view of the house before she picks it up.

"I'm fine, Cabe."

"'Kay. Love you."

She laughs. "Is that it?"

"I'm trying to behave like a good cop."

"He's tricky. I'm heading home. You wanna stop by for the details?"

"Yeah."

"I'm calling Baker now, and then Captain. I'll see you at my place."

Janie makes the calls and reports the events, and Captain makes sure she knows this is a classic case of "fucked-up authoritative egomaniac syndrome."

She made up the term herself.

And then Captain says, "I'm not too worried about the chem fair trip since you'll be with Mrs. Pancake all the time, but be very careful at that party, Janie. I'm guessing he gets off on getting the girls drunk, maybe taking advantage of them then, while the party's going on. Keep your wits about you."

"I will, Captain."

"And do some research on date-rape drugs. I've got some pamphlets on it that I want you to read."

"Yes, sir."

9:36 p.m.

Janie arrives home, steaming with a new hatred for Mr. Durbin. What a manipulator. She'd like to get inside his dream sometime. Turn it into a nightmare.

Ten minutes later Cabel slips in and looks at her all over. Gives her a hug. "Your shirt smells like his after-shave," he says, eyes narrow. "What happened?"

"I did my job," she says.

"And what did he do?"

"Here. Sit here. Pretend you're working on chemistry formulas." She acts it out for him.

"Fucker."

"And then he tried to tell me I was a bad girl to think he'd ever want to touch me. Even though he just did."

Cabel closes his eyes. "Sure," he says, nodding. "That's how he keeps them quiet."

"That's exactly what I thought as he patronized all over me while leaning against the door so I couldn't get out."

Cabel paces.

Janie grins. "I'm going to bed. You can let yourself out when you're through with that."

February 17, 2006, 7:05 p.m.

Janie sits on the living-room floor of Desiree Jackson's house for the study date. A handful of Chem. 2 classmates surround her. They get right down to work on formulas.

Whenever anyone brings up Mr. Durbin's name, the other girls gush over him. Janie fakes it, easing questions about Mr. Durbin into the conversation as carefully as she can. But nobody has anything bad to say about him.

10:12 p.m.

Janie packs up her books and notes, sighs, and goes home with nothing new besides rave reviews of Mr. Durbin. Everybody loves the guy.

A night of studying, wasted. She knows this stuff by heart.

ROAD TRIP

February 19, 2006, 12:05 p.m.

It's snowing.

Hard.

The chemistry students pack their project and their overnight bags into the fifteen-passenger van in the school parking lot while Mr. Durbin paces outside, his gloved hand holding a cell phone loosely to his ear. His hair is thick with snow. He talks in spurts, his words dying in the blustery wind.

Everybody tumbles inside the van, excited and nervous. The students congregate on the front three bench seats.

Except Janie.

Janie takes the fourth bench seat.

Alone.

Shivering.

Mrs. Pancake, shrouded in a full-length, lilac, puffball, goose-down winter coat, peers anxiously out the front passenger window at Mr. Durbin and the blowing, drifting snow.

"We should cancel," she mutters to no one in particular. "It's only going to get worse the farther north and west we go. Lake effect."

The students speak in hushed voices.

Janie pleads with the weather to lighten up. As much as she hates these class trips, she knows she needs this one.

Finally Mr. Durbin blows into the driver's seat with a gust of snow and freezing cold wind. He starts up the van.

"The fair's secretary says it's clear and sunny up north," he says. "And the latest weather reports show this band of snow is isolated to the bottom half of lower Michigan. Once we get past Grayling we should have clear skies."

"So we're going?" Mrs. Pancake asks nervously.

Mr. Durbin winks at her. "Oh yes, my dear. We're going. Put on your seat belt." He puts the van into drive and plows through the snowy parking lot. "Here we go!"

The students cheer. Janie smiles and checks her backpack for supplies. She has everything she needs to get her through the next thirty-six hours. She pulls out *Harry Potter and the Order of the Phoenix*, along with her book light, and dives in.

5:38 p.m.

It takes more than five hours to get to Grayling when it should have taken three. But at least the snow has stopped. The school van limps into a Wendy's parking lot.

"Eat quickly and get back in here," Mr. Durbin hollers. "We have six hours to go. We'll have to set up early in the morning—they're closing the gymnasium at midnight, reopening at six a.m. I suggest you try to get some sleep in, people."

Janie perks up.

Stays far away from Mr. Durbin. She's still pissed about the other night at his house, although she knows she has to get past her contempt. Funnily enough, Mr. Durbin seems to hover around Janie even more when she tries to avoid him.

He slips in step with her as they enter the restaurant, but she ignores him and heads for the bathroom.

Everyone else heads for the bathroom too.

Janie calls Cabel.

"Hi, uh, Mom," she says.

Cabel snorts. "Hello, dear. Did you make it through the blizzard?"

"Yeah. Barely." Janie grins into the phone.

"Anything yet?"

"Nope, not yet. We still have six hours to drive. It's going to be a long night."

"Hang in there, sweets. I miss you."

"I—I love you, Mom."

"Call me when you get a chance. If anything happens."

"I will."

"Love you, Janie. Be safe."

"I will. Talk to you soon."

Fifteen minutes later they are back on the road.

Nobody sleeps.

Figures, Janie thinks.

She takes a nap while she can.

12:10 a.m.

In the hotel room with Janie are three other girls. Stacey O'Grady, Lauren Bastille, and Lupita Hernandez. The four of them chat and giggle softly for a few minutes, but growing tired, they fall into bed, the alarm set for 5:30 a.m.

1:55 a.m.

Janie is sucked into the first dream. It's Lupita, her bed mate. Janie can feel Lupita, twitching in the bed next to her.

They are in a classroom. Papers fly around everywhere.

Lupita frantically scoops them up, but for each paper she picks up, fifty more fall from the ceiling.

Lupita is frantic.

She looks at Janie. Janie stares back, concentrating.

"Help me!" Lupita cries.

Janie smiles encouragingly. "Change it, Lupita," she says. "Order the papers to come to a rest in a pile. It's your dream. You can change it."

Janie concentrates on delivering the message to Lupita. Slowly, Lupita's eyes grow wide. She reaches out her hands to the papers, and they float gently down into a neat stack on Lupita's desk. Lupita sighs, relieved.

Janie pulls herself out of the dream.

Lupita is no longer twitching. She is breathing steadily, deep, calm breaths.

Janie grins and rolls over.

Waits patiently for the one she needs.

2:47 a.m.

It's Lauren Bastille this time.

They are in a room of a house that looks vaguely familiar to Janie. Folding chairs are set up in a circle. People are sitting and standing all around. Some are laughing and falling over. Everyone is drinking some sort of pink

143

punch; some dip their hands into the punch bowl and slurp.

All the people, except Lauren, look fuzzy. Janie can't see any faces, no matter how hard she tries to focus.

Lauren dances in the center of a circle. Her shirt is off and she twirls it as she stumbles around, laughing, wearing just a black bra and jeans.

Someone joins her.

He strips his shirt off and grabs Lauren.

Everyone claps and cheers as the guy pulls Lauren to him. They kiss and grind as the music pounds in the background.

Hip-hop music.

Janie watches in horror as the guy removes Lauren's clothing and shoves his jeans down to his knees. The guy pushes Lauren to the floor, falling on top of her, their drinks spilling everywhere, and the rest of the group begins making out and tearing off one another's clothes. Then they pile up on top of Lauren until people are stacked to the ceiling. Lauren is screaming, muffled. She's being crushed to death.

Janie's numb. Her body shakes. She's had enough, but it's too horrible. She can't escape. She tries to pull herself away, but the nightmare is too strong.

Janie tries to scream, but she knows she can't.

Look at me! she cries mentally to Lauren. *Ask me to help you!*

But this nightmare is out of control. Janie can't get Lauren's attention. She can't pull out of it. She watches in horror as

Lauren fights, tearing uselessly at the people on top of her, shouting, "No! Stop! No!"

Janie summons all her strength and tries to pause it. Tries to scan the room again. It's not working.

Until.

With a final, heroic effort, Janie manages to pry her eyes off of Lauren. Looks around the room.

There.

In the kitchen.

Laughing and drinking, watching the craziness, like it's a football game or something.

Someone has a cell phone out.

A strange expression on her blurry, laughing face.

When Lauren screams, everything goes black. Janie is paralyzed, blind. She hears Stacey mumble, "What the heck?" and feels Lupita groan and shove her head under her pillow. And Janie waits for three things:

Lauren to stop breathing so hard.

Her own sight to return.

And to feel something.

Anything.

It takes a very long time for all three things to happen.

Morning comes too quickly.

February 20, 2006, 8:30 a.m.

The chem team finalizes their display. It's a DNA helix, with posters theorizing how cloning could safely be done with humans.

Janie doesn't care much about it. She lets the real chem geeks do all the work.

Which they probably preferred anyway.

Mrs. Pancake arrives with doughnuts, and they sit and wait for the observers and judges to come by. Everyone looks exhausted, including Mr. Durbin.

Janie excuses herself and goes into the restroom.

Calls Cabel.

Tells him everything about Lauren's dream.

They hover together in grim silence over the phone.

"Be careful," Cabel says for the hundredth time.

"I just can't understand how no one seriously reported it or followed up on it, unless they were all too wasted to remember," Janie murmurs. "There must have been something in that punch. Captain told me to study up on date-rape drugs. I think she nailed it."

"Sounds like it, J."

The door to the restroom opens and Lupita walks in, waving cheerily at Janie.

"I've got to go," Janie says quietly as she returns Lupita's wave, and hangs up.

4:59 p.m.

The team packs up the display. They walk away with white third-place ribbons. Not bad for a stupid theory and a hundred brazillion Popsicle sticks.

By nine p.m. everyone is dozing in the van. Everyone but Janie and Mr. Durbin, that is. Janie struggles and pulls herself out of a variety of ridiculous dreams. Thankfully the silly ones are the easiest to pull out of.

She snacks and tries to sleep between dreams.

Finally Mr. Durbin pulls over along the highway. The sleeping troupe rouses to see what's going on.

"My dear Rebekkah," Mr. Durbin says to Mrs. Pancake, "can you drive for a bit? I'm falling asleep."

Mrs. Pancake glances nervously at Mr. Durbin.

"Just for an hour or so," he says. Pleads.

"Fine," she says.

Mr. Durbin climbs out of the van and enters the rear sliding door. "Somebody, go sit up there with Pancake, will you, please? I need to stretch out."

He drops into the backseat with Janie. "Hey," he says. His eyes travel up and down her cloaked body.

"Hey," Janie says, trying to appear interested, but then gives it up and looks out the window into the night. Watches the snow beginning to fall lightly around them. Wonders if something terrible is about to happen.

That she'll be discovered shaking and blind because of Mr. Durbin's dreams, or that he'll try something creepy in the dark nether regions of the van.

Neither one sounds especially good right now.

Mr. Durbin stretches and yawns. By the time they've gone ten miles, he's snoring lightly next to Janie, his legs splayed out into the aisle, his upper body tilting and sliding an inch at a time toward Janie.

She's trapped.

She wills herself to stay awake and keep her wits about her. Manages to last an hour, maybe.

11:48 p.m.

Janie startles awake.

The van is humming. Everyone else is asleep except Mrs. Pancake up front. Everyone too exhausted to dream.

Janie looks at Mr. Durbin.

His shoulder is against hers. His hand on her thigh.

Janie blanches. Shoves his hand away. Shrinks farther into her little corner and turns her back to him.

He doesn't wake up.

He doesn't dream.

Useless piece of shit, thinks Janie.

3:09 a.m.

The van pulls into Fieldridge High's parking lot. All the students' cars are blanketed in nearly two feet of snow.

Janie shoves Mr. Durbin awake.

"We're here," she says gruffly. She just wants to go home to bed.

The group stumbles out of the van.

"See you in the morning, bright and early for school," Mrs. Pancake calls out into the crisp night as the students wearily shove the snow from their windshields.

Janie calls Cabel.

"Hey. I've been waiting up for you," he says, sounding worried. "Are you safe to drive?"

"I can't imagine any people will have their windows open on a night like tonight," she says.

"Come to me."

"I'm five minutes away."

Janie falls into Cabel's arms, exhausted. Tells him about Mr. Durbin in the backseat of the van.

He leads her to the bedroom, helps her into one of his T-shirts, and whispers in her ear as she falls asleep, "You did great work."

Closes his bedroom door.

Makes his bed on the couch.

Lies awake, pounding his pillow in silence.

February 21, 2006, 3:35 p.m.

Janie, dark circles under her eyes, and Cabel, concerned look on his face, sit in Captain's office. Janie snacks on almonds and milk as she relays the events of the chemistry fair adventure.

"It looked sort of like Durbin's house," she says. "His living room."

"But you couldn't see anyone's face?" Captain presses her.

"No," Janie says. "Just Lauren's. She's the one who was dreaming." She wrings her hands.

"It's okay, Janie. Really. You've given us a lot of information."

"I just wish I had more."

Cabel reaches over and squeezes her hand. A little too tightly.

Afterward, Janie heads home, checks on her mother, grabs dinner, and hits the sack. Sleeps twelve hours straight.

February 27, 2006

Cabel calls Janie on the way to school.

"I'm right behind you," he says.

"I see you," she says, and smiles into the rearview mirror.

"Hey Janie?"

"Yeah?"

"I've got a huge, terrible problem."

"Oh no! Not that horrible toenail fungus that takes six months to cure?"

"No, no, no. Much worse. This is shocking news. Are you sure I should tell you while you're driving?"

"I've got my headset on. Both hands on the wheel. Windows rolled up. Go for it."

"Okay, here goes . . . Principal Abernethy called me this morning to let me know I'm in the running for valedictorian."

There is silence.

A rather loudish snort.

And guffaws.

"Congratulations," she finally says, laughing. "What ever are you going to do?"

"Fail every assignment from today onward."

"You won't be able to."

"Watch me."

"I am so looking forward to this. Oh, and also? You suck."

"I know."

"I love you."

"Love you too. Bye."

Janie hangs up and laughs all over again.

Second-hour psych is a sleeper. Janie stumps Mr. Wang with a question on dreams, just for the hell of it. Leaves him stuttering, so she isn't late to Mr. Durbin's.

For the week leading up to the party, Janie continues to play the woman scorned in front of Mr. Durbin, and he appears to eat it up. In fact, the more she avoids him, the more he comes up with excuses to call her to his desk after class or requests she stop by after school.

She remains aloof, and he goes out of his way to compliment her—on the test, her experiments, her sweater. . . .

March 1, 2006, 10:50 a.m.

"You still coming an hour early on Saturday?" Mr. Durbin asks Janie after class.

"Of course. I promised I would. Stacey and I will be there at six."

"Excellent. Hey, I couldn't do this big party without you, you know."

Janie smiles frostily and walks to the door. "Of course you could. You're Dave Durbin." She slips out and heads to English lit, with boring old Mr. Purcell. He is the epitome of moral character.

Study hall outright sucks. By the time it's over, Janie has too much information about nothing important. And when she lifts her head, she sees the shadows of feet and legs next to the table.

"Are you okay, Janie?" It's Stacey's voice.

Janie clears her throat, and a crashing noise comes from the section of the library to the left. Stacey whirls around and gawks. Janie can't see what's happening, but once she can feel her lips, she smiles. *Cabel's up to something*, she thinks.

She sits up as if she can see, and, indeed, her vision is returning somewhat now. She coughs and clears her throat again, and Stacey turns back to her.

"Sheesh. What a klutz. Anyway, I came over to make sure Saturday at six was right."

"Yep," Janie says. "That's just you and me heading over to Durbin's house to set up. Are you comfortable with that?"

Stacey gives her a quizzical look. "Why wouldn't I be?"

"I have no idea, but you can't be too careful these days, can you?"

Stacey laughs. "I guess. Well, we've got the appetizers all figured out. I hope he has enough electrical outlets, 'cause there's going to be a shitload of Crock-Pots. Of course, we could always use Bunsen burners."

"Good one! Hey, I've got a list of desserts and snacks. Phil Klegg is bringing something called 'dump cake,' and I just don't even want to know what's in there."

They chitchat a little about the party and about the chem. fair, and when the bell rings, Stacey hustles off. Janie peers between the bookshelves and, after the library empties out, sneaks over to where Cabel's sitting.

"Are you okay?" she whispers, giggling.

"Me? Oh sure. You might have to carry me out of here, though."

"What happened?"

"I created a distraction."

"I gathered that."

"Step stool, encyclopedias, floor."

"I see. Well, I can't thank you enough."

"Sure you can. Help me flunk enough tests, so I drop out of the 'torian range."

"Can't you just tell Abernethy that you have a reputation as a dumbshit to keep up, and you don't want the attention?"

"Flunking is more fun."

Janie shakes her head and laughs. "Maybe the first few times. But I bet you won't be able to handle it after that."

"I'll take that bet."

Janie puts her hands on her hips. "All right. After the fourth flunk of something quizlike or weightier, you will struggle and fail to flunk number five. That's my prediction. Loser pays for our first real date."

"You're on. Start saving your money."

SHOWTIME

March 3, 2006, 10:04 a.m.

Chem. 2 is buzzing with excitement, and the students goof around more than anything else. Mr. Durbin lets them. They all did relatively well on the most recent test, the chemistry fair garnered them higher-than-expected results, and everyone is jazzed for tomorrow's party. Mr. Durbin is practically giddy himself, and when Coach Crater stops at the door, because of the ruckus, he pokes his head in.

"Must be a Chem. 2 party coming up," he remarks, eyeing the students one at a time.

"Tomorrow night, Jim," Mr. Durbin says. "Stop by, if the wife will let you out." They chuckle.

Janie's eyes narrow at the comment, but she goes back to her text book. She's looking for a formula—the formula for date-rape drugs. Not that she'd find it in a high-school text book. There's a recipe for disaster. Yet maybe a clue lies within.

But when Mr. Durbin starts walking around to the various stations, she flips her book to the current lesson page and pretends to read. Mr. Durbin pauses for a moment behind her, but she ignores him. He moves on.

In PE, they're in the weight room for four weeks, learning the machines and proper free-weight stance. Dumbass calls Janie up to the front to help demonstrate.

"How much weight do you want, Buffy?"

Janie looks at him. "Well, sir, I guess that depends on the exercise you'd like me to demonstrate."

"Right!" he says, like it was a teaching question. Janie's expression doesn't change. "How about the bench press," he says.

"Free weights or machine?"

"Oooh, aren't you smart? Let's start with free weights."

She gives him a long look. "Are you spotting me or not?"

He chuckles for the audience, like he's doing a magic trick. "Of course I'll spot you."

Janie nods. "All right, then. One-twenty's good."

He laughs. "How about we start at, say, fifty or something."

"One-twenty is fine for a single lift." She bends down and starts adding the weights herself. The students are highly amused, at the encouragement of Coach Crater.

Janie tightens the caps and lies down on the bench, the bar above her chest. "Ready?"

She waits for him to get into spotter position, and grips the bar. Closes her eyes. Concentrates, breathes, until she no longer hears the distraction around her. She pushes up on the bar, holds it a moment, then lowers it evenly to just above her chest and presses upward with all her might. She holds it for a few seconds, and then lets it down slowly in the cradle. "Eighty-five for reps," she says, making the proper adjustments. She presses eight reps, replaces the bar when she's finished, and only then does she tune back in to the room. It's pretty quiet.

Coach Crater is standing, looking down at her, amazed, stupid grin on his face. Janie turns to her side and sits up on the bench, and then walks to the back of the room. Later in the class, she's getting in half her workout for the day. Bonus.

"Asshole," she mutters to Coach Crater as she leaves at the end of class.

"What?"

She keeps walking.

Five minutes into study hall, a paper wad from Cabel hits her in the ear. She rolls her eyes. Opens it up.

Stacey, it says.

Janie looks up. Stacey's head is on her books. Her eyes are closed. Janie bites her lip and nods at Cabel. He gives her an encouraging smile.

Her blood is still pumping from PE. She feels strong. She slept well, ate well . . . has everything going for her. Now all she needs is for Stacey to—

She grips the table, and they are in Stacey's car. Stacey's driving furiously, as before. From the backseat, the growl, the man, his hands gripping Stacey's neck.

Janie wonders if this is the best shot she'll have or if she should wait. She decides to take it, in case Stacey wakes up before they get to the woods.

Stacey's driving erratically. Janie concentrates and squeezes her hands into fists, pumping them before they become numb, focusing on pausing the dream. It's slowing, and Janie tries to turn to look at the man. But the dream speeds up again.

She can't do both things at once. Janie concentrates again on pausing the scene, and she knows her power is limited. One broad push of energy, and the scene slows and stops. She stays perfectly focused, turns slowly, evenly. Sees the look of horror on Stacey's face, sees the man's hands around her neck, his arms, and then slowly, slowly, turns to see the face of the man.

He's wearing a ski mask.

Janie loses concentration, and the dream goes to regular speed again. Damn it. They hit the ditch, the bushes; the car rolls, comes to a stop. Bloody Stacey climbs out through the broken windshield and runs, the rapist follows, into the woods, and Janie tries again to pause the dream, when he grabs Stacey. Janie tries with all her might. But she can't do it. The rapist has Stacey, she trips, he falls on top of her, and then it ends abruptly, just where it always does.

She wishes now she'd tried to help Stacey change it. Next time, maybe.

She actually hopes there isn't a next time.

Fifteen minutes later, when she can see and move again and the library has emptied out for the day, Cabel spends a moment squeezing her tightly, and she can't explain how amazing that feels. He walks with her to the parking lot, takes her home, and goes back for her car, like last time.

Janie eats and drinks, checks on her mom, and falls asleep on the couch.

He's there when she wakes up. Reading a book, his feet on the coffee table.

"Hey," she says. "Time?"

"A little after eight p.m. How you doin'?"

"Good," she says.

"Your mom here?"

"In the bedroom, like always."

Cabel nods. "Captain wants to meet with us in the morning to go over tomorrow night."

"Yep, I figured."

"I'm worried about you, Janie."

"About the dream? It was only worse because I paused it."

"You did it? Cool!"

"Yeah. But I didn't see anything."

"Oh well. What I'm actually worried about is tomorrow night."

"Please don't be. It'll be fine. Eighteen students there, Cabe. I'm not going to get drunk. I'll have a beer or something in my hand, so Durbin doesn't get suspicious, but I'll just fake like I'm drinking it. I'll eat a lot before I go too."

"I hope Captain has an escape plan. You'll have your phone?"

"Yep. And all I need to do to call you is push one button."

"I'll be close by."

"Not too close, Cabe, okay?"

Cabel tosses his book on the table. "You can still back out of this, you know, Janie."

Janie sighs. "Cabe, hear me: I. Don't. Want. To. I want to do this. I want to stop this guy! Why can't you understand that?"

Cabel cringes. "I can't help it. I can't stand the thought of that creep touching you, Janie. What if something awful happens to you? God, I just hate this."

"I know." Janie pushes up on her elbows and sits up. The last thing she wants right now is a fight. Changes the subject. "Is Ethel back home?"

"Yes, she's in the driveway."

"Thank you. I don't know what I'd do without you."

"I wouldn't worry about it if I were you."

Janie leans against him. Strokes his thigh with her fingertips. "Why do you put up with this?"

Cabel relaxes and twirls a string of Janie's hair. "Well, duh. Because one day you'll be really rich and famous, I bet. Your own TV show, people throwing money at you just to get you to change their dreams. I'm holding out for the money. After that I'm outta here."

She laughs. "Did I tell you I benched one-twenty in

PE today? And then I called Coach Crater an asshole."

Cabel roars in laughter. "He *is* an asshole. And one-twenty is probably a national record or something. That's almost more than you weigh."

"The national record is more than two hundred for my age and size category. But I'll take it."

They talk for an hour, and then Cabel heads home. Tomorrow they'll meet again in Captain's office.

After Cabel leaves, Janie pulls out her chemistry book; curiously searches through a chapter; uses her cell phone to peruse the Internet for an hour or so, until she finds the information she's looking for on date-rape drugs; and goes to bed.

March 4, 2006, 9:00 a.m.

Baker and Cobb join Cabel and Janie in Captain's office. Janie meets Cobb and says hello again to Baker.

Captain goes through the schedule for the evening. Janie will arrive at six p.m. along with another girl. The rest of the guests will come at seven.

Captain gives Janie a thin, sexy cigarette lighter, one of the newly popular, old-fashioned flip-top kinds. "It's not a real lighter, Janie. If you flip the lid open, it sends a distress signal to Baker and Cobb outside the house. They'll call your cell phone first, just in case it's an accident, and don't panic if that happens. Answer if it happened by mistake. But just try to keep the lighter in your pocket, and it'll be fine. If you don't answer your phone, they'll move in and call you once again. If you do not pick up, they will come in for you.

"In other words, if you're in trouble, flip open the lighter lid. Put your cell phone on vibrate and wear it in your underwear if you have to, but you must answer that phone if nothing's wrong. If you do not answer, they will assume trouble is afoot. Is that perfectly clear?"

"Yes, sir," Janie says.

"Good. Let's talk about drinking. Believe me, Durbin's going to be watching that everybody has a drink in hand."

Janie looks at her suspiciously. "You're not going to arrest me or anything if I have a drink in my hand, right?"

Captain raises an eyebrow. "Not unless you do something stupid. But I think you should carry around a beverage, yes, so nobody gets suspicious. I don't encourage drinking on the job, though."

"Okay . . . and no setting my beverage down at any time, right? No keg, no punch bowl, no mixed drinks."

Captain nods, impressed. "You've done your homework on date-rape drugs, I see. Good job." She pulls a small package of date-rape drug testers from her desk drawer and hands them to Janie. "Are you familiar with these?"

Janie smiles, reaches inside her bag, and pulls out an identical package.

"Excellent." Captain nods. "Cabel. What's your job?"

"Watching in agony, sir."

Captain suppresses a smile. "I'd make you stay home if I didn't know you'd sneak out, anyway. While you are watching in agony, feel free to take note of anyone who comes or goes that's not on the list."

"Thank you," Cabel says meekly.

"Baker and Cobb, you clear on procedure?"

"Yes, sir," they say together.

"Great. You two may go."

Baker and Cobb slap Janie on the back, like she's one of the guys, give her the thumbs-up, and head out. Janie grins.

Captain turns to Janie.

"Tonight is not the night to get sucked into any drunk

person's dream. Try and steer clear if you can. If you can't, we'll deal with that later. I do understand you can't control the actions of other people, so don't panic if it happens and you get stuck."

Janie nods.

"And be safe. Follow your gut. You're smart. You have a terrific sense of intuition. Use it like you have in the past, and we'll all walk away just fine. All right?"

"Yes, sir."

"Any questions?"

"No."

"Good. Call me if you think of any," Captain says. "And, Janie, I have never been more serious. Use that panic lighter if you need it. Don't be a martyr and don't think you can handle this job alone. We work as a team. Got it?"

"Got it. I'm ready, sir."

"And a reminder. This could be nothing more than just an ordinary party. Our goal is to find and arrest a sexual predator. Not to bust the guy for serving a few drinks to minors. We can always get him next time for that. Like I said, use your intuition and judgment."

"I will."

"Cabel. Any questions?"

"No, sir."

"Get on out of here, then. I'll see you sometime in the next twenty-four hours, I expect. Damn, I hate this job."

10:09 a.m.

Janie makes her crème-de-menthe bars and puts them in the refrigerator, and then makes lunch. Cabel stops by and mopes around uselessly, unable to talk about anything. Janie finally sends him away.

"Be careful, baby," he says, kissing the top of her head.

Janie's quiet.

And he's gone.

2:32 p.m.

Janie lights her relaxation votive candle and sits still on her bed, clearing her mind, meditating. Preparing herself. She mentally runs through her profile sheets. All the events that led up to today. And then her mind strays to Stacey's car dream. She goes through it, step by step. She knows there's a connection between the dream and Mr. Durbin, but how? Did Mr. Durbin actually rape her? Janie thinks about Lauren. Wishes she could have focused on the faces in her party dream, but they were blurred beyond recognition. And if Lauren has nightmares about the party, why doesn't she have qualms or reservations or downright contempt for the host? Why didn't the anonymous caller follow up with another call to Crimebusters Underground?

She dozes for an hour, asking herself to figure out

the connection between the dreams and this party tonight.

Herself says no.

When she wakes up, Janie takes a shower and puts on tight jeans and a low-cut V-neck sweater. She adds a hint of makeup and ties her hair back, low, in a ribbon, leaving a few wisps out to frame her face. She grabs a snack and a glass of milk, making quick work of them, and brushes her teeth. Puts on some lip gloss.

It's showtime.

5:57 p.m.

"I'm pulling up to the house. I'll see you after," Janie says.

"If you get a chance to call me . . . safely . . . you know . . ." Cabel's voice is anxious.

"I will if I can. Love you, Cabe."

"Love you, Janie. Be safe."

They hang up. It's a warm night for early March, and the snow is gone, leaving muddy yards, puddles, and potholes everywhere. Janie parks on the street, double-checks her pockets, grabs her dessert, and takes a deep breath, then strips off her coat and tosses it on the passenger seat next to her. Never hurts to have an excuse to get out of the house. She bought a pack of cigarettes earlier and leaves them in the coat pocket.

Janie closes her eyes momentarily, gets into her character, and gets out of her car. She sees the tail end of Baker's "soccer-mom" minivan down the street, and he flashes the brake lights at her. For some reason that makes her feel tremendously more confident, and she smiles in his direction, knowing he can see her with his high-powered binoculars. Cobb is stationed on the next street, with a partial view of the back of the house. She doesn't look for Cabel, but she knows where he is—around the corner.

She slams her car door and walks up the driveway to Mr. Durbin's front steps, hoping Stacey shows up soon. She knocks and hears footsteps. Mr. Durbin opens the door and ushers her in.

"Hey, Janie," he says, letting her in and closing the door behind her.

"Looking good, Mr. Durbin," Janie says with a grin, glancing around. He's rearranged the furniture, set up extra folding chairs, and added two card tables to the great-room area.

"You too, Janie," he says, looking her up and down. "You can call me Dave outside of school, you know."

She turns and gives him her full attention, and watches his eyes move to her chest. "Dave," she repeats. "I should probably keep this refrigerated," she says, indicating her dessert. "Mind if I poke around your kitchen so I know where to find things? I figure I can help you out with the food and drink distribution once everybody gets here."

"Be my guest," he says. Not a hint of apprehension.

Strike one, Janie thinks. He follows her and shows Janie where he keeps extra dishes, glasses, silverware, and napkins.

"The fridge is packed pretty tightly," he says, "but there's room on the bottom shelf, if you move a few beer bottles around." He stands behind her while she bends over and shoves her dessert inside. "You want a beer or something? I'm making punch, too."

"Are you having one?" she asks.

"Sure."

On the fridge, holding—what else?—two snapshots of Mr. Durbin himself, is a magnet. *The* magnet, with the Fieldridge Crimebusters hotline number. Janie's heart pounds. *He screwed himself*, she realizes, thinking of the blurred, anonymous person in the kitchen, making the call.

Swiftly, Janie pulls out two bottles of beer and Durbin shows her where the bottle opener is, when from the hallway comes none other than Mr. Wang. He's barefooted and his hair is wet.

"Mr. Wang," Janie says, controlling her surprise. "I didn't know you were here."

"Ms. Hannagan," he says with a nod.

Mr. Durbin grins. "So formal, you two. Chris, Janie," he says. "Janie, you want to grab a beer for Chris? I've got to get this punch going. Chris came early to help me with the tables and chairs, and then we ended up in a rather competitive game of one-on-one. Basketball," he adds.

"I see. Well it's very nice to see you, uh, Chris." She winks and he looks nervous.

"Likewise, Janie."

Janie hands Mr. Wang a beer. He looks around the room to see what needs to be done, and finally, rather helplessly, he goes to the stereo and starts rummaging through the CDs. "I'll take my usual spot as the DJ," he says.

The doorbell rings, and Stacey lets herself in with a shriek of "Woo hoo!" Janie raises her eyebrow.

"Hey, Stacey," Janie says when Stacey brings her Crock-Pot to the kitchen's island.

"Janie!" Stacey smells like beer already. "Are you ready to party?"

Mr. Wang has Coldplay on now, and he cranks the volume. "Now I am," Janie says, holding up her beer. Wonders how wild the party has to get before Mr. Wang moves to hip-hop.

She takes the paper cups and beverage napkins to the great room, where Mr. Durbin is pouring a bottle of cranberry juice into a punch bowl that already has a clear liquid in it. He adds a bottle of Ruby Red Squirt to the mixture as Janie sets up the table display, and then he goes to the sink to get an ice ring, and plops that in as well.

Janie opens the package of napkins and lays them out in a spiral design. "What goes on the other table?" she asks.

Mr. Durbin stirs the punch with a ladle. "I figured we'd put some munchies out there. You want to be in charge of keeping that going?" He takes a cup and pours a little of the punch in it, tasting it, nodding approval.

"Sure. I saw some stuff on the counter. I'll get serving bowls and put those things out here."

"I have a little apron you can wear if you'd like," he says under the noise of the music, so only she hears it.

Janie raises her eyebrow and glances at him. He's grinning.

Stacey comes over to the punch table. "Is this the same stuff you made at the last party, Dave? And if it is, I should probably test it, don't you think?" She gives him an innocent look.

"Absolutely," he says, pouring a glass for her.

Janie goes to the kitchen and begins to distribute the munchie items into various-size bowls. When she takes them to the table, Mr. Wang is downing some punch too. "How about it, Janie?" Mr. Durbin offers her a glass.

"After my beer," she says with a grin. "What's in that stuff, anyway?"

"Just a little vodka. You can't even taste it," he says.

"But you can feel it." Stacey giggles.

Mr. Wang is beginning to loosen up now, and by seven p.m., Mr. Durbin, Mr. Wang, and Stacey are bantering comfortably.

Janie takes advantage of the moment to pour some of her beer into the sink before the doorbell starts ringing. It doesn't stop for the next hour. She plays hostess.

8:17 p.m.

Everyone has arrived, and the party is beginning to pick up speed. Janie works the kitchen, arranging the dishes as people bring them in. She spreads the dining table with the appetizers, and at one point, uses the excuse of looking for an extension cord to scout around the other rooms in the house.

She's in his office/den off the kitchen when Mr. Durbin finds her. "Whatcha doin', hot stuff?"

She turns and grins, hiding her guilt from snooping. "I'm looking for an extension cord, so we can keep all the appetizers warm. Do you have one handy?"

He's standing very close. "Downstairs," he says. "Come on, I'll show you," he says. His voice is sexy.

She licks her lips, looking into his eyes. "Show me

the way," she says, pointing with her beer. Her heart thuds heavily at the thought of going downstairs with Mr. Durbin.

The door to the basement is through the kitchen. It's a finished basement, with a full bar, big-screen TV, and two giant fluffy-looking couches. Janie follows Mr. Durbin through a door into a workshop with a small worktable. On it sits a Bunsen burner and several flasks and beakers. On the shelves above it are a variety of chemicals. Janie strolls over to it and rapidly checks them out. "Oh cool! I want a lab table in my house," she whines.

He comes up behind her and puts his hand lightly on her waist. His thumb rolls gently, back and forth on her side. She leans into him slightly as her eyes scan the shelves.

And then he's taking her arm and pulling her with him. "I gotta go mingle," he says. They climb the stairs, to where the music is loud again. "Here's the extension cord," he says, handing it to her. "Come on, you need to have some fun now. Get out of work mode and enjoy yourself. It's a party, for Chrissake." He grins and pinches her ass. "Get some of this punch, Janie," he says, holding up his empty cup. "I promise you, you'll lighten up and have a great time."

He sets his cup on the kitchen counter, and after Janie has the network of plugs configured, so that nobody could possibly trip over all the cords, she glances around, grabs the cup, and makes a beeline to the bathroom.

There's a line. She doesn't want to wait.

She slips down the hall, peers into a dark bedroom, and sneaks inside, locking the door. Turns on the lamp on the dresser, and pulls a package out of her pocket. She rips open the package, takes out a round paper circle, and tips the near-empty cup, so a single drop pauses on the rim of it and splashes on the paper.

She rubs it in and waits.

Thirty seconds, and it's dry.

And nothing happens.

She takes a second paper circle and tries again.

Still nothing.

"Hm," she says. She crumples up the papers and shoves them into her pocket, replaces the package to the other pocket, grabs the cup and her beer, and goes back out to the party.

Janie tosses the cup in the trash and peeks inside quickly. Two empty fifths of Absolut lay at the bottom of the trash bag. She closes the wastebasket and washes her hands. She can hear the students, louder now, laughing and dancing.

9:45 p.m.

Janie's bored. And dying of thirst. All the soda is in open two-liter bottles left unattended, and maybe she's paranoid, but Janie doesn't trust the tap water because it has one of those filter things on it. She looks at the warm, half-full bottle of beer in her hands. Knows it's probably the only safe thing in the house, since it hasn't left her hands from the moment she opened it.

Many of the guys have gone downstairs to watch basketball, and a few girls too. But most of the girls are swaying and laughing in the great room, and Mr. Wang is entertaining them with his dance moves. Four girls sit on the floor playing Texas hold 'em. The food has hardly been touched. Everybody has a beer or a cup of something in hand. Janie stabs a meatball with a toothpick and nibbles at it. It's delicious, but only succeeds in making her even more thirsty.

And then Mr. Durbin emerges from the kitchen with a fresh bowl of punch. He makes a general announcement, and half the girls gather around, holding out cups. He generously ladles punch, and he pours one for himself, and Mr. Wang too. Mr. Wang, sweating from dancing, downs his punch and lifts his cup to Janie, who sits on the couch making small-talk with Desiree. Desiree is nicely half-drunk, not too slobbery, and Janie has really learned to like her. She's smart and funny.

Mr. Wang pours a second cup of punch and brings it over to Janie. "For you," he says. His black eyes are shiny. He sits next to Janie and leans back, closing his eyes.

"Long day, Chris?" Janie says when Desiree slips away to refill her glass.

He opens a lazy eye. "Long and hard," he says wickedly.

Janie nods. "Thanks for sharing." She holds the cup in her hand. Listening to the music. It's the Black Eyed Peas. "Got any Mos Def?" Janie asks.

"Mos' definitely," Mr. Wang says, laughing at his own stupid joke. He lunges unsteadily toward her. "Whoa," he whispers, catching himself on her thigh. "I'll just get that on later. Hey, you know, lighten up already, princess," he says, tilting his head quizzically. "Your type is supposed to get plastered at these kinds of parties. You know, free booze." He leans in and sniffs her neck. "You smell terrific," he says. He rests his sweaty head on her shoulder.

My type? Janie burns. She can't help it. She wants to kick Mr. Wang's ass. "Jesus Christ," she mutters. "You wanna know what the trailer trash like, huh, Chris?"

"Not all the trailer trash. Just you." He's slurring his words.

"Wait right here for me, then," she says, shrugging Mr. Wang's head off her shoulder and trying to hold in her disgust. "I'll be back."

"Oh yeah," he says, grinning happily.

Janie mingles her way to the bathroom with her untouched punch and stands in line. By the time she gets in there, she hears the clumping of a dozen feet coming up the stairs. Mr. Durbin's explaining boisterously that somebody's gotta be the one to start eating, because the girls aren't doing it. She locks herself in the bathroom and does the drink test again.

Spreads the drop of punch on the paper.

Waits thirty seconds.

Watches it change to bright blue.

Her stomach lurches.

Rooffies.

She dumps the punch into the toilet, and flushes.

Searches through the drawers and cupboards for bottles of liquid, powder, or pills. Finds nothing. Janie could call in the cops now, she knows. But she doesn't have proof that it was Mr. Durbin who did it. What if one of the other students brought it in? If Janie can find the drugs, it'll help even more in prosecuting the bastard. She remembers the last case, how frustrated Cabel and Captain were when Baker and Cobb busted the drug scene before Cabel could get the location of the cocaine. Janie wants proof. Wants to get this done right. *It's still early*, she thinks as she rifles through Mr. Durbin's things. *I can find it.*

Heads across the hall and searches the bedroom. Slips into the other bedroom and searches it, too. Nothing, nothing. *Back downstairs*, she thinks.

It's hot, and Janie's really thirsty now. She takes a sip from the beer in her hand. It's flat and warm. But it'll have to do. Captain won't blame her for trying to stay hydrated, will she? After all, Janie's just being smart. She knows from experience that she can easily handle two beers without it affecting her.

Janie eases past a few guys standing in the kitchen and heads to the basement. The TV and lights are all on. But everyone is upstairs now. She hopes they stay that way. She slips into the dark room with the lab table, and peers at the labels, moving the big items to search for smaller containers. She doesn't see what she's looking for. Frustrated, she turns and goes back upstairs. Dumps out the rest of her stale beer. Grabs a fresh one from the refrigerator and a paper plate from the food table.

She loads up her plate, taking a long, thirsty swig of her beer between the meatballs and the veggie tray. *It's gotta be here somewhere*, she thinks. *Maybe Durbin's bedroom? But the door's closed, and it's right off the great room. I'd be seen. And what if he's in there?*

Janie shoves half a meatball in her mouth, and chews. Delicious. She noshes on a carrot stick, and moves toward the great room. Finds a place in the crowd to stand and eat. Thinking. Thinking hard.

People are out of control.

She munches, eyes like slits, looking for Mr. Durbin and Mr. Wang. The roar of voices is growing stronger every minute. The music grows steadily louder.

She concentrates on her watch. Makes her eyes focus. 11:08 p.m.

11:09 p.m.

Squeezes between two guys with her plate of food and her beer, and discovers what they are so engrossed in watching.

Janie stares at the scene. She's feeling the effects of the beer, even though she only sipped a little from the first and drank half of the second. Still, she's dying of thirst and doesn't dare to drink anything else. She chugs down the rest of this beer, and then eats quickly, knowing she still has work to do. Knowing things are getting a little crazy.

She glances at the punch bowl. Nearly empty. Students are sprawled around the room, sitting on one anothers' laps, making out. A few are sitting alone, a vacant, dazed look on their faces. And in the middle of the room, where everyone else's eyes are riveted, Mr. Wang and Stacey O'Grady are dirty dancing. Very dirty. Mr. Wang's shirt is off, and his muscles bulge and shine with sweat. Janie's eyes wander over his body, and she is surprised to find him suddenly, strangely, attractive.

Stacey is completely toasted. She can hardly stand up. Janie reminds herself to keep an eye on her. People are slurping the dregs of the punch, like it's a desert oasis. Mr. Durbin comes from the kitchen with more.

Janie lets her eyes wander lazily as she eats. She's feeling tired. Mellow. The guys who aren't otherwise occupied head back downstairs, tripping and shoving their way to the TV. Janie's head is buzzing now, and she's surprised—she's only really had one beer. She should eat more, she tells herself, to stop the buzz.

Back in the kitchen, she loads up her plate a second time, head starting to spin. She leans against the counter, hoping it will pass.

And then she stops.

A distant thought—a nudge. Something she was about to do. She pictures it.

Looks up on top of the refrigerator.

A can of paint stripper.

A bottle of Red Devil Lye.

That's . . . something, she thinks, screwing her eyes shut, trying to concentrate. But her brain isn't working right. *That's . . . that's it.* She knows she needs to remember it, but now she can't imagine why.

Janie's buzzing hard now, and she's not sure she likes it. She sits down on the floor and digs into the food, trying to stop spinning, finish the food on her plate, feeling sleepy. *Gotta call . . .* The thought pops into her head, but leaves again just as quickly. Someone trips over her leg, and Janie drags her body up off the floor and stands, and then tries to remember why she stood up at all. She shakes her head, attempting to clear her mind, and gets dizzy, nearly falls, bumping into somebody else who looks vaguely familiar. She laughs at herself and remembers what she has to do. She picks up her plate and throws it in the garbage can. Two points.

Her skin is tingling as she wanders around, checking out the students on the couches who are in various stages of pre-sex. Janie watches them curiously. And then she thinks maybe she's in somebody's dream. She stumbles around the great room, knowing that if she really is in somebody else's dream, no one else can see her. Stacey and Mr. Wang are gone. Too bad, because Janie wanted to watch them dance some more.

Twelve something in the morning. Janie's eyes linger on the clock, not quite comprehending the position of the hands.

There's a sudden ruckus in the room, and Janie rouses herself, trying to remember where she is and why she is there. She stands up from the floor, wondering how she got there in the first place. Mr. Durbin is standing by the door, handing Coach Crater a drink. Crater drinks it down in one shot, and Janie is impressed. He's cute, too, she thinks. And she is still so thirsty. She wanders to the kitchen, looks in the refrigerator, and sees her dessert. "Hey," she says, her tongue feeling strangely thick. "I should set that out." She reaches for it, misses on the first try, but gets it on the next one—after serious concentration. And someone is touching her bum.

She stands up and sets the dessert on the counter, so she doesn't drop it. "Whoa," she says, laughing.

"Mm," says Mr. Durbin. "Here, I brought you something to drink. You look thirsty." *He's slurring his words too*, thinks Janie. It must be his dream. Janie remembers that she should be glad to be in Mr. Durbin's dream, but she can't remember why.

She smiles gratefully. "Thank you so much," she gushes, and holds up the cup, feeling like there might be something she's supposed to know about it, but her thirst overwhelms her. "Is everything tipping just a little bit in here?" she asks, laughing like it's the funniest thing she's thought of all day, and then puts the cup to her lips. The punch slides down her throat, cooling it. "I thought all the punch was gone. Mm, oh god. That's so yummy," she says.

And then Mr. Durbin's pushing her back against the counter and kissing her, and she's feeling his hot tongue on hers. She starts kissing him back, because that's what feels right. The fuzziness in her brain grows.

"I gotta go . . . ," she says suddenly, pulling away.

"No, you don't have to go."

"I mean, to the bathroom," she says seriously.

"There's one in my bedroom," he says, his eyes hungry.

"Oh, cool. Do you still have that porn magazine in there?" Janie hesitates too late, wondering if she was supposed to say that, but she can't remember why she shouldn't.

"Lots of them," he says. "Not that I need them with you here."

"Huh." She follows him through the dazed and half-naked crowd. He stops to grab another glass of punch, and gives her another one too. On the way to Mr. Durbin's bedroom, Janie waves at Coach Crater. "Hey," she says, turning back to Mr. Durbin. "Wasn't Stacey here? Before?"

"She's still here, Janie." His words are deliberate, like he's concentrating. "She's fucking Chris in the other bedroom, so we can fuck in here." His words sound like slow-motion, matter of fact, and Janie is certain she's in his dream now.

He shows her to the bathroom, and she decides maybe she should close the door, even though she doesn't feel like it. It's so much work. But that's weird, because if it's Mr. Durbin's dream, why would she be in a room where she can't see him?

She sits down on the toilet, her head heavy. Something seems wrong, but she doesn't know what it is. She sits there for a long time, in a half-dream. She almost falls asleep, she's feeling so warm and mellow. And in her mind, she's whirling through memories that pop in and out of her brain.

She hears a knocking sound, far away.

"Just go home, Carrie," she mumbles.

She can't seem to open her eyes.

She leans to the right, and there's a cool, comfortable wall to rest her cheek on.

There is another knocking sound. But this one turns into a car's-engine knock, and Stacey's driving. There's going to be a man coming any second from the backseat, Janie remembers, and then he's there, gripping Stacey around the neck. *His hands are sexy*, she thinks.

"Come on, Janie, don't be shy," she hears from far away, and Janie rouses herself.

"What?" she says.

"Come on out, sweetheart. We're all waiting for you."

It must be Cabel. He sleeps a lot. And then she remembers she's sitting on the toilet, and she chuckles silently to herself and finishes up.

She drinks a long drink from the bathroom tap. She's so thirsty. She wants milk. Milk always makes her feel stronger. She turns to leave, but the door is gone. It's just a wall now.

She scratches her head.

Looks around.

Laughs.

It's on the other wall.

Stumbling, Janie bumps against the door, trying to push it, and finally tries pulling it. It opens, and Mr. Durbin is on the bed. There are three girls from class with him, and he's taking their clothes off as they lie there.

Janie finds this fascinating.

But now she remembers that she wants milk, so she walks carefully out of the bedroom, trying not to bang into anything.

Mr. Wang is standing by the slider door in his underwear, letting the cool air inside the house. "That feels great," Janie says. She breathes it in.

It smells like cigarette smoke.

She stands there, spinning. There it is again. That thing that feels funny.

Coach Crater comes down the hallway toward them, as Janie tries to remember why she came to the kitchen.

"Hey, there you are, Buffy," he says.

Surprisingly he's wearing jeans and a shirt, although his shirt is open and his chest hair shows.

Janie looks around. Walks back to look in the great room. Everyone is practically naked. *How bizarre*, she thinks, and goes back to feel the cold air again.

And then Coach Crater grabs her by the shoulders and turns her toward him. He plants a big wet kiss on her mouth. And moves on.

He's tripping as he walks to get more punch.

She remembers that she doesn't think she likes him. But maybe that's not really true.

It's so hard to decide what is true.

She smells more cigarette smoke, and she has an urge to go outside to have a cigarette. So she goes to the door.

Outside on the deck, it's dark. Mr. Wang follows her out there, in his Calvin Klein briefs. Janie breathes in the cold air. She holds on tightly to the railing when Mr. Wang starts touching her. "I smelled smoke," she explains, but she doesn't see anyone smoking.

And then Coach Crater comes out too. Mr. Wang is kissing her neck, and Coach is telling her how hot she is and feeling her up, and he says something about bench pressing.

Finally she remembers why she hates him.

And she remembers that she smelled smoke, but no one is smoking.

Then, in her mind, while the two men kiss and touch her, is Miss Stubin.

Telling her something.

Janie struggles to listen. She remembers liking that old lady for some reason.

Cigarette, Miss Stubin says in Janie's mind.

"I need a cigarette," Janie whispers.

Use your lighter, Miss Stubin says. *In your pocket.*

"I need a cigarette," Janie says louder. "Now."

Coach Crater goes inside and comes back with a joint. "How's this, Buffy?"

"Okay." Janie takes the joint with a shrug and reaches into her pocket. She didn't know she had a lighter. Maybe the old maid put it there.

And then the words register, from what Coach Crater just said.

Janie.

Does not like.

To be called.

Buffy.

Janie reels back against the deck's handrail, stumbling, grabs Coach's arm off her breast, wrenches his elbow around so he twirls and faces the other way, and she kicks him, hard, in the kidneys. "Don't call me 'Buffy,'" she says mildly. "Ever again."

His feet splay sideways and he lands with a thud on the wet deck, moaning.

Janie pulls the lighter from her pocket as Mr. Wang stares. She examines it, puts the joint in her mouth, and pulls back the lid.

She tries lighting it.

No fire comes out.

She tries it again.

Mr. Wang is confused, looking at Coach Crater, who is groaning and barely moving on the deck.

"Get me a fucking lighter that works, or I'll beat the shit out of you, too," she says to Mr. Wang, and sinks to the deck, exhausted. When her hip starts buzzing, she just figures it's one of those weird things that have been happening all night.

She looks at Coach Crater. He's sprawled every which way. His hands are reaching. Reaching for her leg. She watches them, like it's not happening to her. She focuses on his fingers, thinking how weird fingers are. Like little animals, all their own.

He's wearing a strange, square ring. She wants it, sort of. It looks cool, like he belongs to something.

Mr. Wang returns with a lighter just as Janie's hip buzzes again. Maybe she'll have to have her whole leg amputated, she thinks sadly. That would really suck.

She lights the joint and inhales the smoke. Holds it in. Lets it out slowly. Mr. Wang falls to the deck next to her and starts kissing her cleavage.

She doesn't like that, she decides. He's in her way. She's trying to smoke a joint here.

She makes a peace sign with her fingers, marveling over them. Then, when Mr. Wang grabs her nipple in his mouth, she stabs him in the eyeballs.

She learned that somewhere.
She doesn't know where.

Mr. Wang swings his fist wildly, crying out in pain. He catches her on the jaw, her head flies back and hits the deck's rail, and she blacks out. The joint burns down between her fingers.

NOT ALL RIGHT

March 5, 2006, 6:13 a.m.

Janie is dreaming. She's dreaming Stacey's dream, over and over again, and she's dreaming that she can't pull out of it. She tries. Hard. But she's stuck on the rapist in the backseat.

Over and over again, the dream pauses on the rapist's hands. And then she sees it.

She gasps awake and sits up wildly, even though she's numb. "Oh god," she croaks, her voice gone. She can't see. But someone is talking, rubbing her hands, her arms. Soothing her with his voice. She's breathing hard, in and out, and she cries hot tears, because all she wants is to open her eyes. But they feel open.

"I need my glasses," she cries out in a broken voice. "I can't see."

"Janie, it's me, Cabel. I'm right here. I have your glasses, and you'll be able to see in a few minutes. You're safe." His voice breaks and he pauses. "You're safe. Just sit back and rest. Wait for it. You'll see shadows in a minute, and then everything else will come back, okay?"

Janie slumps back.

She shudders, but she can't remember why.

She tries to breathe, in and out.

"What time is it?" she whispers.

"Six fifteen."

She hesitates. "Morning?" she guesses.

"Yes, morning."

She breathes again. "What day?"

There is a short silence. "It's Sunday morning, sweetheart. March 5."

"Is Stacey O'Grady in this room?"

"No, baby. She's down the hall."

"Is the door closed?"

"Yes."

Janie doesn't understand, but her brain is still fuzzy, like her eyes. And then slowly, bits of things return.

And she knows there are two very important things she told herself to remember, even when everything was out of control. She speaks slowly.

"Cabel?"

"Yes?"

"GHB. Mr. Durbin cooked it up himself out of paint stripper and lye. That's my guess. I looked it up before. I didn't see him do it. But he has the stuff. And, obviously, the ability."

She breathes, exhausted. "Only twelve hours before it's out of the body. Urine tests. Everyone. Every fucking one."

She doesn't see him blink.

"Good job," he murmurs, and he's on the cell phone. Talking gibberish.

She's trying hard to focus. There's something else. What is it? She can't remember.

He stops talking on the phone, and he's rubbing her arm.

And then she remembers. "Meatballs," she says. "The drug was in the punch, but I swear to god I didn't drink the punch. Not that I can remember. I tested it. The tests are in my jeans pocket. Right side." She pauses. Sobs a little. "He must have put the GHB in the meatball sauce, when I was in the bathroom, testing the punch. God, I'm so stupid."

She drifts off, still blind, and sleeps fitfully for a few hours.

9:01 a.m.

Janie blinks awake. The light above her on the ceiling is blinding.

"Where the hell am I?" she asks.

"Fieldridge General," Cabe says.

She sits up slowly. Her head aches. She holds her hands to her face. "What the fuck," she says.

"Janie, can you see?"

"Of course I can see, you asshole."

He does a double take, looks at the woman next to him, who chuckles, and he closes his eyes briefly. "You feel like talking?" he asks carefully.

She blinks a few more times. Sits up. "Where the fuck am I?" she asks again.

Cabel plants his forehead in his hands. Captain steps to the plate.

"Janie, do you know who I am?"

Janie peers at her. "Yes, sir."

"Good. And who is this?"

"Cabel Strumheller, sir. You remember him, don't you?"

Captain buries a grin. "I do, now that you mention it." She pauses. "What do you remember?"

Janie closes her eyes. Her head aches. She thinks for a long time.

They wait.

She finally speaks. "I went to the party at Durbin's house."

"Yes," Captain says.

Cabel slips out of his chair and begins to pace the floor.

"I remember setting up the food." She strains against the fuzziness.

"That's good, Janie. Take your time. We've got all day."

Janie pauses again. "Oh god," she says. Her voice shivers and falls.

"It's okay, Janie. You were drugged."

A tear slips down Janie's cheek. "That wasn't supposed to happen," she whispers.

Captain takes her hand. "You did everything right. No worries. Just take your time."

Janie sobs quietly for a moment. "Cabe's gonna be mad," she whispers to Captain.

"No, Janie. He's fine. Right, Cabe?"

Cabel looks at Captain and Janie. His face is ashen. "I'm fine, Janie," he manages to croak.

Captain captures Janie's eyes. "You know this, Hannagan, goddamnit. Anything that happened as a result of you being drugged against your will is not your fault. Right? You know your stuff. And you know that. And whoever did anything to you will go to jail, okay? Not your fault. Don't turn soft on me, Janie," she adds. "You're a strong woman. The world needs more like you."

Janie swallows hard and turns her head away. She wants to bury herself under the covers and disappear. "Yes, sir."

"Would it help you remember if I mention some of the names?" Captain asks.

"Maybe," Janie says. "I don't remember much. Just wisps of things."

"Okay. Let's start with Durbin. What happened with him."

Janie sighs. Then she opens her eyes wide. "GHB," she says, and sits up. "GHB."

Cabel gives Captain a frightened look. "Settle," she says to him, under her breath. "She doesn't remember talking earlier. It's normal." She turns back to Janie. "What about GHB, Janie?"

Janie thinks. "I tested the first punch," she says. "I thought for sure there'd be rooffies in it. But it was clean. Just vodka. That's what he told me."

"Good job. You are a professional."

"And then people started getting weird. Durbin brought out a new bowl." The wisps are a little stronger.

Captain sits quietly, letting her think.

"He made all the guys come upstairs from the basement. They were watching TV. He said they should start eating, because the girls wouldn't do it."

Captain scowls, but holds in her disgust.

"And then . . ." She thinks. "Wang gave me some punch and gave me shit about being trailer trash. What a fucker," she says, her eyes stinging. She cries for a minute, and then pulls it together.

"He was messed up by then," she continues. "I thought something was going on. So I took the punch he gave me and tested that—I didn't drink any. The paper turned blue, and I flushed it all down the toilet." She closes her eyes again.

"I went downstairs," she says slowly. "I checked the chemicals on his lab table, and I didn't see the ones I was looking for—GBL and NaOH. Those two chemicals combined make GHB, a drug-facilitated, sexual-assault weapon. I studied about it, like you told me to."

Captain nods.

"But when I got upstairs, I remembered seeing some bottles on top of his refrigerator. Paint stripper and lye. The same chemicals that create GHB."

"By then I was paranoid and worried. All the soda was in open two-liter bottles, and I didn't even want to get a glass of water, because he had one of those water-filter things on the tap, and I thought he maybe put the drug in it. So I grabbed a beer—I'm so sorry, Captain—and drank it sort of fast, but I had food by then too. And a beer, honestly, is not too much for me. I don't know what happened," she says, crying again, covering her face. "I screwed up, didn't I?"

Captain closes her eyes. "No, Janie. You did fine. We should have thought to send you with some individual water bottles or something."

Cabel stops pacing and rests his forehead against the window. Bounces it against the glass a few times. Mutters unintelligibly.

Captain carefully continues. "You told us a few hours ago, something about the meatballs. Do you remember that?"

Janie is silent. Confused. "I don't remember meatballs."

Captain nods at Cabel. He looks quizzically at her, then he nods. He dials his phone. Talks to someone. Eventually hangs up.

"GHB, confirmed in the meatballs and in the veggie dip," he says. "Jesus Christ." He takes off his rugby, leaving his T-shirt on. Begins pacing some more. "I didn't know you could put it in food."

"Apparently Durbin wanted to cover his bases," Captain says quietly, eyeing Cabel carefully. She turns back to Janie. "Is there anything else you remember? Don't worry if you can't. I expect that's probably about it."

Janie remains quiet for a long time. Finally she says, "This is weird, but I know Coach Crater raped Stacey. Not this time. Last semester."

The room rings in silence.

"How do you know, Janie?" Captain asks.

Janie hesitates. "I can't prove it."

"That's okay. Give me your hunch. Remember? We can't solve crimes without leads."

Janie nods. Tells her the car dream Stacy's had since last fall. And then tells her about pausing the dream and not being able to see the face. "But I saw his hand," she says. "In the dream he's wearing a square fraternity ring. I remember seeing the same ring on Crater's right hand last night."

Silence.

And more silence. Cabel makes another phone call.

Captain ventures another question with an almost-smile on her face. "Do you remember when you activated the panic button?"

Janie looks at her. Shakes her head no.

"So you don't remember beating the shit out of Crater and Wang?"

Janie stares. "What?"

Captain smiles. "You were amazing, Janie. I hope someday you remember it. Because you should be very proud of yourself, like I am of you."

Janie closes her eyes.

Finally she says, "Cabe, can you step out for a minute?"

He gives her a fleeting look, then goes.

"Captain," Janie says, "did anything happen? You know. With me?"

Captain holds her hand. "Nothing below the belt, kiddo. When Baker and Cobb found you, your sweater was off your shoulder. That's it. The doctors did an exam. You stopped them, Janie."

Janie sighs in relief. "Thanks, sir."

6:23 p.m.

Cabel drives Janie to his house.

"Twenty-one positives on the GHB, Janie." Cabel's voice is harsh. "Everyone at the party was drugged. Durbin even drugged himself. Rumor has it, the drug is known to enhance stamina." He pauses. "Ewww." They both shudder. "When Baker and Cobb and the backup crew arrived, Durbin had three female students in his bed with him."

Janie is quiet.

"He's going to jail for a long time, Janie."

"What about Wang?"

"Him too. Sadly, he raped Stacey before Baker and Cobb got there. They found his DNA. She asked for the morning-after pill. She doesn't remember anything that happened last night." Cabel's hands grip the steering wheel. His knuckles are white.

Janie's quiet. "Fuck," she says.

She should have done better.

Done better for Stacey.

Janie's headache dulls by evening. She eats everything Cabel gives her, and then declares herself fit. "Stop babying me already," she says with a cautious grin. She knows Cabel hasn't slept.

Cabel gives her an exhausted, lost look. Sucks in a breath as his face crumbles. He nods. "I'm done," he says. "Excuse me." He walks out of the room, and Janie hears him in his bedroom. Yelling into his pillow.

Janie cringes.

Realizes now she was in way over her head. And, maybe, so was Cabel.

After a while he is quiet. Janie ventures a peek into his bedroom, and he's asleep on his stomach, fully clothed, glasses flung on the nightstand, his arm and leg hanging off the edge of the bed, tears still clumping his eyelashes, cheeks flushed. Not dreaming.

Janie kneels next to the bed, smoothes his hair from his cheek, and watches him for a very long time.

March 9, 2006, 3:40 p.m.

The uproar at Fieldridge High School has settled, some. Janie's three substitute teachers are less than exciting. Which is okay, because Janie's having trouble concentrating, anyway. Not because of Mr. Durbin's party. But because of what happened after, with Cabel.

After school Janie's at home, lying on the couch, staring at the ceiling, when Carrie pops her head inside Janie's front door.

Janie sits up and forces a smile. "Hey. Happy, happy. Did you do anything fun for your birthday?" She hands Carrie a small gift bag that's been sitting on the coffee table for days.

"The usual. Nothing fancy. Stu thinks I should go register to vote, of all things. I hope he's joking."

Janie attempts a laugh, even though she feels numb. "You should register to vote. It's your right as an American."

"Did you?"

"Yes."

"Oh my *god*!" Carrie exclaims, slapping her hand to her mouth. "Did I miss your birthday?"

Janie shrugs. "When have you ever remembered it?"

"Hey! That's not fair," Carrie says, grinning sheepishly. But Janie knows it's true. So does Carrie.

Not that it matters.

That's just the way things are with them.

Carrie ooohs over the CD Janie bought her. And they are okay. But Janie knows that things are changing rapidly.

Carrie doesn't stick around long.

Janie has no plans for the evening.

Or for the rest of her life, it seems.

She calls Cabel.

"I miss you," she says to his voice mail. "Just . . . had to tell you that. Um, yeah. Sorry. Bye."

But Cabel doesn't call back.

She knew he wouldn't.

"I need a break." That's what he said that Monday after the hospital, when he tried to touch her but couldn't.

NOTHING LEFT
TO LOSE

March 24, 2006, 3:00 p.m.

Janie is in a daze now. It's been nearly three weeks. She goes through her classes like a zombie. Goes home after school. Every day, alone.

Alone.

It's fierce. There's so much more to miss now. Being alone before Cabel was much easier than being alone after Cabel.

He doesn't sit nearby in study hall anymore, either. Doesn't call. Doesn't check on her when she gets sucked into dreams.

He can't even seem to look at her. And when it happens

by accident—in the hallways, the parking lot—his face gets a stricken look, and he hurries on, without a word.

Away from her.

Even at the follow-up meeting with Captain, she was alone. Cabel met with Captain separately.

Janie drives home, windows open on this fresh spring day, with nothing to lose.

3:04 p.m.

She stops for an elementary-school bus whose red lights are blinking. She looks at the children, crossing the street in front of her. Wonders if any of them are like her.

Knows they probably aren't.

And then.

She's taken by surprise. Blind, sucked into a little kid's dream.

Falling, falling off a mountain.

Janie gasps silently.

Her foot slips from the brake pedal.

The bus horn wails and screams.

She grips the steering wheel frantically and struggles with her mind to focus. Pulls herself out of the dream as Ethel strays dangerously close to the street-crossing children.

Slams a numb, heavy foot on the brake and blindly reaches for the keys in the ignition.

Ethel conks out and dies as Janie's sight returns.

The bus driver gives Janie a hateful look.

The children scurry to the side of the road, staring at Janie, eyes wide in fear.

Janie, horrified, shakes her head to clear it. "I'm so sorry," she mouths. She feels sick to her stomach.

The bus roars away.

While the drivers who are lined up behind Janie begin honking impatiently, Janie struggles to start Ethel.

Bawling her eyes out.

Hating her life.

Wondering what the fuck is going to happen to her, wondering how she's going to get through life without killing somebody.

She makes it home.

Wipes her face with her sleeve.

Walks determinedly into the house. Goes directly to her bedroom, tossing her coat and backpack on the couch without stopping.

Until she gets to her closet.

Janie pulls out the box and sits on her bed. Dumps

it all out in a pile and picks up the green notebook.
Recklessly opens it up. Reads the dedication again.

A Journey Into the Light
by Martha Stubin

This journal is dedicated to dream catchers. It's
written expressly for those who follow in my
footsteps once I am gone.

The information I have to share is made up of
two things: delight and dread. If you do not want
to know what waits for you, please close this
journal now. Don't turn the page.

But if you have the stomach for it and the desire
to fight against the worst of it, you may be
better off knowing. Then again, it may haunt you
for the rest of your life. Please consider this in all
seriousness. What you are about to read contains
much more dread than delight.

I'm sorry to say I can't make the decision for you.
Nor can anyone else. You must do it alone. Please
don't put the responsibility on others' shoulders.
It will ruin them.

Whatever you decide, you are in for a long, hard
ride. I bid you no regrets. Think about it. Have
confidence in your decision, whatever you choose.

Good luck, friend.

Martha Stubin, Dream Catcher

Janie ignores the rush of fear and turns the page. And then turns the blank page. And she reads.

> You've read the first page by now, at least once. I imagine you spent some time on it, perhaps days, deciding if you wanted to continue. And now here you are.
>
> In case your heart is thumping, I'll tell you that I'm starting with "Delight." So you can change your mind if you wish to go no farther. There will be a blank page in this notebook before you reach the information I've titled "Dread." So you'll know and not turn the pages with fear.
>
> I am sorry to have to place this fear in your heart. But I do so for my own reasons. Perhaps you'll understand when you are through reading.
>
> But for now, there is still time to go back and close this notebook. If you choose to go on, please turn the page.

3:57 p.m.

Janie turns the page.

> Delight
>
> You have experienced a bit of this already, I imagine. If not, it will come.
>
> With time comes both success and failure. Some of your best successes as a dream catcher will not be realized for many years.

By now you've discovered that you have more power than you once knew. You have the ability to help someone change a dream to make it better. Less frightening, perhaps. Or even a complete change, such as turning a monster into a cartoon.

What you need to know before you assist in altering someone's dream is that not all dreams can be altered. Your power is strong, but there are a few dreams stronger than you. Please don't expect you can change the course of the world.

That said, I, Martha Stubin, have been in the dreams of many successful individuals. They arrived at success only after their dreams changed. Can I take credit for these things? Of course not. But I was a factor in the future of many a businessperson. While I will not reveal names, as the individuals are still alive at the time I write this, I might ask you to think about the computer industry, and that will give you a clue.

You have the ability to influence the unconscious mind, my dear dream catcher.

Marriages have been saved.

Relationships rekindled.

Sports events won.

Lives lived in confidence rather than fear.

Because our power is motivating, and gives momentum and ownership of changes to those who dream of failure.

This is a most redeeming job when things go right.

And you can change a community.

You are a rarely gifted individual.

You can use your power to help create or restore peace in a troubled community—whether it's a school, a church, a place of business, or a government entity. You have more power to solve crime than anyone with a badge.

Do not forget this.

As you hone your skill—your gift—you will be able to assist the law in ways the keepers of them cannot imagine. And in ways that are impossible, in their minds. You have tremendous power to do good.

Use it if you dare.

You will never be without a job. Think big. The country's many law enforcement agencies will get wind of your existence. Travel the country—maybe even the world. Seek out others with various gifts, who work underground, like you.

Let me take it a step deeper. Into your own heart.

With practice, you will master your own dreams.

Some of you might not dream.

That will come with time.

You can dream to work out the problems you face, and you will dream to find the refreshing love you long for in an isolated world.

And the loved ones you lose along the path
of life will live forever, if you use your power.
You'll never say good-bye for long. Just until
you sleep again. You can bring them back
to you.

This has been the most redemptive factor for me.
It's what has kept me alive beyond my years. I will
die happy, even after a life of distress.

Do not overlook the positives of this factor, once
you view the rest.

And now, when you turn the page, you will find
the next one blank. Following it are the things I
wish I didn't have to tell you. Use your judgment
right now to decide if you wish to go on.

4:19 p.m.

Janie buries her head in her hands, and goes on.

Dread

My eyes water as I write this section.

There are things about yourself you may not want
to hear or know.

Will they help you?

The answer is yes.

Will they hurt you?

Absolutely, yes.

Rights and Obligations

First of all, let us revisit how you change people's dreams.

Because you have the power does not always mean you have the right or the obligation.

And because you have the power of manipulation, some of you will use that to hurt people.

I can't stop you from doing that.

I can only implore you to resist the temptation to hurt others in this fashion.

It's been done.

And it's been ugly.

People die.

Here are some facts you should know:

- THERE IS NO "CURE," SHOULD YOU SEE THIS AS A DISEASE. UNTIL THE REASON FOR THE DREAM CATCHER'S GIFT IS DISCOVERED, THERE WILL BE NO CURE.

- I'VE SPENT FIFTY YEARS TRYING TO CHANGE IT. AND ALL I CAN DO IS CONTROL IT— SOMETIMES.

Driving

You might already be aware of the hazards of driving. Perhaps you've had a rare incident. And

you're still alive. But because of the stray
possibilities—even with the windows closed,
I must add—you are a time bomb.

It's happened before.

You've seen it in the papers, haven't you?

Somebody blacks out on the highway. Crosses
the line. Kills a family of three in the oncoming
lane.

Dream catchers. Catching, by accident, the
dreams of the sleeper in the car next door.

Right through the glass windows of both cars.

It happens.

It has happened.

And I've never forgiven myself.

Don't drive.

You risk not only your life, but the lives of
innocent others.

You can ignore me.

I'm asking you not to.

If you wish to continue, please turn the page.

4:53 p.m.

Janie—shaking, crying, remembering the school children—continues.

Side Effects

This is the hardest section. If you make it through this, you are done.

And maybe you won't think it's as bad as I made it out to be. I hope for that.

There are several side effects of being a dream catcher. You've experienced the caloric drain by now. It gets worse as you age.

The stronger you are, the more prepared you are, the better you'll fare. Have nourishment with you at all times. Dreams are where you least expect them.

The more dreams you enter, the more you can help people. This is true; it's the law of averages.

But for a dream catcher, the more dreams you enter, the worse the side effects.

The faster you decline.

You must work at controlling which dreams you enter.

Practice pulling out of them, as I explained in the many files of cases I've participated in.

Study them.

Practice the moves, the thought processes, the relaxation exercises.

However, you must realize by now that it's a catch-22. Because the more practice you get, the harder it is on your body.

You must choose your dreams carefully, if you choose to use your gift to help others.

Or there is the alternative.

Isolation.

If you isolate yourself, you might live a normal life. . . . As normal as isolation allows, of course.

And now.

You can still stop reading here.

Your last chance.

5:39 p.m.

Janie looks away. Reads that part over again. Her head is pounding. And she continues to the bitter end.

Quality of Life

I knew, personally, three dream catchers in my life, besides myself. I am the last one alive. At the time of this writing, I know of no others. But I am convinced you are out there.

I'll tell you first that the handwriting in this journal is not from my hand. My assistant writes to you in this book, because my hands are gnarled beyond use.

I lost the function of my hands and fingers at age thirty-four.

My three dream-catcher friends were thirty-five, thirty-one, and thirty-three, respectively, when they could no longer hold a pen.

That is what these dreams are doing to you.

6:00 p.m.

Tears stream down Janie's face. She holds her sodden sleeve to her mouth. And continues.

And finally.

What I see as the worst.

I was eleven at the time of my first dream catch. Or at least, that's as far back as I can recall.

The dreams came few and far between at first, as I expect they did for you, unless you shared a room with someone.

By high school the number of dreams grew.

College. In class, the library, walking across campus on a spring day . . . not to mention having a roommate. In college dreams are everywhere. Some of the worst experiences you'll ever see.

And then, one day, you won't.

You won't see.

Because you'll be completely, irreversibly, heartlessly blind.

My dream catcher acquaintances: Twenty-three. Twenty-six. Twenty-one.

I was twenty-two.

The more dreams you enter, the sooner you'll be blind.

You suspected already, didn't you.

Perhaps you've already lost some of your vision.

I'm so sorry, dear friend.

Choose your profession wisely.

All the hope I can add is this:

Once you are blind, each dream journey you take will bring you back into the light, and you will see things in the dreams as if you are seeing them in life.

These dreams of others are your windows. They are all the light you'll see. You will be encased in darkness except for the dreams.

And since that is the case, I ask you, who would

not live for one more dream? One more chance to see your loved one as he ages, one more chance to see yourself if he dreams of you.

You don't have a choice.

You are stuck with this gift, this curse.

Now you know what lies ahead.

I leave you with a note of hope, and it is this: I don't regret my decisions to help others through catching dreams.

Not a single instance would I take back.

Now is a good time to sit and think. To mourn. And then to get back up.

Find your confidant. Since you are reading this, you have one. Tell him or her what to expect.

You can get to work. Or you can hide forever and delay the effects. It's your decision.

No regrets,

Martha Stubin, Dream Catcher

Janie stares at the book. Turns that page, knowing there's nothing more. Knowing it's not a joke.

She looks at her hands. Flexes her fingers. Sees them, their wrinkly knuckles and short fingernails. The way they bend and straighten. And then she looks around the room.

Takes off her glasses.

Thinks hard and knows the answer already. The dreams, the headaches, Miss Stubin's gnarled hands and blind eyes. Janie's own failing eyesight. Janie knew.

Knew it for a while now.

She just didn't want to think about it. Didn't want to believe it.

Maybe Cabel knows already, she thinks. His stupid eye charts. Maybe that's really why he needs a break. He knows she's falling apart. And he can't handle one more problem with Janie.

Janie is so stunned she cannot cry anymore.

She grabs her car keys and rushes to the door before she remembers.

Miss Stubin killed three people in a car crash because of a dream.

Janie looks at Ethel through the window, and then slowly she falls down to the floor, sobbing as her world comes to an end.

She doesn't get up.

No.

Not that night.

March 25, 2006, 8:37 a.m.

Janie is still on the floor in the living room, near the front door. Her mother steps over her once, twice, unalarmed, disappearing again into the dark recesses of her bedroom. She's seen Janie asleep on the floor before.

Janie doesn't move when there is a knock on the door. A second knock, more urgent, does nothing to her.

And then words.

"Don't make me break open the door, Hannagan."

Janie lifts her head. Squints at the door handle. "It's not locked," she says dully, although she tries to be respectful.

And Captain is there, in Janie's living room, and somehow, in the small house, she looks so much bigger to Janie.

"What's going on, Janie?" Captain asks, alarm growing on her face as she sees Janie on the floor.

Janie shakes her head and says in a thin, bewildered voice, "I think I'm dying, sir."

Janie sits up. She can feel the carpet pattern indented deep in her cheek. It feels like Cabel's nubbly burns. "I was going to go see you yesterday," she says, looking at the keys on the floor next to her. "I was going out the door, and then it all hit me. The driving. And the everything. And I just . . ." She shakes her head. "I'm going blind, sir. Just like Miss Stubin."

Captain stands, quiet. Waits patiently for Janie to explain. Holds her hand out to Janie. Pulls her up, and embraces her. "Talk to me," Captain says gently.

And Janie, who ran out of tears hours ago, makes new ones and cries on Captain's shoulder, telling her everything about the contents of the green notebook. Letting Captain read it herself. Captain squeezes Janie tightly when the sobs come again.

After a while Janie is quiet. She looks around for something to use to wipe Captain's coat, and there is nothing. There is always nothing at Janie's house.

"Did you call into school for your absence yet?"

"Shit."

"No problem. I'll do it now. Does your mother go by Mrs. Hannagan? I don't want the office staff to know that I know you."

Janie shakes her head. "No, not 'Mrs.,'" she says. "Just go with Dorothea Hannagan." When Captain hangs up the phone, Janie says, "How did you know to come?"

She scowls. "Cabel called me. Said you didn't show up at school, wondered if I'd heard from you. I guess he tried calling your cell phone."

So I have to disappear in order to get him to call me. Janie doesn't say anything. She wants, with all her heart, to ask Captain why Cabel won't speak to her. But Janie knows better than to do that. So all she says is, "That was thoughtful."

And then she thinks for a moment. "Did you suspect this? Did Miss Stubin tell you any of this?"

"I knew something was bothering you after you called me a few weeks ago, but I didn't know what. Miss Stubin was a very private person, Janie. She didn't speak much about herself, and I didn't ask. It wasn't my place."

"Do you think Cabel knows?"

"Have you thought about asking him?"

Janie glances up to read her face. Bites her quivering lip to still it. "We're not exactly on speaking terms right now."

Captain sighs. "I gathered that." Carefully she says, "Cabel has his own demons, and if he doesn't get on with killing them soon, I'm going to kick his ass. He's having trouble dealing with some things right now."

Janie shakes her head. "I don't understand."

Captain is silent. "Maybe you should ask him. Tell him what you're going through too."

"Why? So that when I tell him I'm going to be a blind cripple, he'll never want to come near me again?"

Captain smiles ruefully. "I can't predict the future, Janie. But I doubt a few physical ailments would turn him off, if you know what I mean. But nobody says you *have* to tell him, either." She pauses. "You look like you could use some breakfast. Let's go for a ride, Janie," she says.

Janie looks down at herself, rumpled in her clothes from yesterday. "Sure, why not," she says. She takes a few minutes to brush through her hair, and she looks in the mirror. Looks at her eyes.

Captain takes Janie to Ann Arbor. They stop for breakfast at Angelo's, where Captain apparently knows everybody in the place, including Victor, the short-order cook. Victor himself delivers a feast to their table. Janie, not having eaten since lunch the day before, wolfs down the meal gratefully.

After breakfast, Captain drives around the campus of the University of Michigan. "Some of the finest research and medical facilities are here, Janie. Maybe there's something . . ." Captain shrugs. "Keep in mind, Martha Stubin lost her eyesight fifty years ago. A lot has changed in the medical world since then. Don't doom yourself before you know what doctors can do now. And not just your eyes—your hands too. And, perhaps, your dreams. See that building?" Captain points. "That's the sleep study. Perhaps something can be arranged to accommodate you properly sometime. I have a couple friends on campus I trust. They knew about Martha. They'll help us."

Janie looks around at everything. Feels a tiny surge of hope. She and Cabel had planned to come out here a few times over the upcoming summer, once they could be seen together. Now Janie doesn't know what to think. Maybe Cabel would be back.

And maybe he would be scared away again.

Janie doesn't know how many more breakups and fixes she can handle in their relationship. "Why does everything have to be so hard?" she asks out loud. And then she blushes. "Rhetorical question. Sorry, Captain."

Captain smiles. "What made you read it, finally?"

Janie swallows hard. "Now that Cabel won't come near me, I figured I didn't have much else to lose. Joke's on me, huh."

Captain purses her lips as she drives and mutters something under her breath. "Okay," she says, "and how do you feel about being a dream catcher now?"

Janie thinks. "I guess I don't know any different."

Captain gets a curious look on her face. "How does your mother play into this picture?"

"She doesn't."

"And your father . . . ?"

"Doesn't exist, as far as I know."

"I see." Captain pauses. "Are you sorry you read it?"

Janie is quiet for a moment. "No, sir."

They sit in silence, and then Captain points out a few more buildings on the U of M campus. "Do you want to quit your job with me, Janie? Isolate yourself?"

Janie looks at Captain. "Do you want me to quit?"

"Of course not. You're brilliant at it."

"I'd like to stay on if you have more assignments for me, sir."

Captain smiles, and then she turns serious again. "Do you think you can still work with Cabel, even if you don't resume your romantic relationship with him?"

Janie sighs. "If he can handle it without being an ass, I can." And then her voice catches. "I just . . ." She shakes her head and collects her wits, not wanting to cry.

Captain glares through the windshield. Bites her lip. Shakes her head. "I swear to god I'm going to smack that boy," she mutters. "Listen, Janie. Cabel doesn't have much— he has a mother who abandoned him, a father who nearly killed him . . . And now, when he's with you, he desperately wants to keep you safe in his pocket all the time. But he knows he can't. He's got to learn how to handle that."

Janie takes this in. "But, Captain, he couldn't even bear to touch me after the Durbin bust." She starts crying. "It's like he was so disgusted that they had touched me or something. . . ." She reaches for a tissue from between the car seats.

"Jesus Christ," Captain says. "Janie, listen to me. You're a good detective already. You know that in our work, we have hunches and we seek out the answers. You do this so well in your work. Why don't you follow that same line of logic in your personal life? You'll need to talk to Cabel if you want answers. Endless speculation only leads to dead ends."

Janie closes her eyes. Rests her head on the headrest. "I'm sorry, Captain. You're right. I swear I won't let this mess affect my work. Working for you is the best thing in my life. I feel like I can actually make a difference, you know?"

Captain gives Janie's arm a quick squeeze. "I know, kiddo. And I've got big plans for you, if you're game."

"Captain?"

"Yes."

"How am I going to get anywhere if I'm not supposed to drive?"

Captain sighs. "I haven't figured that one out yet."

"Did you know Miss Stubin had a car crash because of a dream? She killed three innocent people."

Captain slows the car and glances at Janie. "I knew from her background check that she was in a terrible car accident once. I didn't know it happened because of a dream." Captain pauses. "She was sixteen when it happened."

Janie sits in stunned silence.

Captain continues. "She was convicted of vehicular manslaughter, Janie. She lost her license and did three years in a women's correctional facility. It would have been more if she hadn't been a minor at the time. This is serious stuff."

Janie's stomach churns. "I almost hit some school kids yesterday," she says softly. "Some little kid on the bus was dreaming."

Captain shakes her head resolutely. "Well. That

settles it. If I catch you driving again, Janie, I'll write you a ticket myself, I swear to god. Meanwhile, if I need you somewhere, I'll drive you or send a car. I don't want you wasting dreams on some damn city bus."

Janie feels like she just got put in a cage. "What about school?" she asks. "I'll have to take the school bus. What am I going to tell people? Cabel will figure it out. This is such shit."

Captain gives her a hard look. "You know what shit is? Killing three innocent people. Think your life is bad now, try living with that." Her voice is harsh.

Janie's quiet.

They head back to Fieldridge.

When Captain's cell phone rings, she glances at it and answers. "Komisky." She pauses. "Yes, I've got her." Another pause. "Yes, she's just fine." She nods, glances sidelong at Janie with a grim smile, and then hangs up the phone.

"Juuust fine," Captain repeats, her lips pressed tightly together in a thin line.

12:36 p.m.

Captain drops Janie off at home and gives her a swift hug. "You call me if you need to talk more about this stuff," she says.

"Thanks, Captain."

"And it's your call, what you want to tell Cabel, if

anything. Be assured it's not my place to tell him unless it directly affects your work as partners, and even then, I'd ask you to do it. As for you not driving, I think Cabel will take that very well. He worries enough about it. Blame me."

Janie waves weakly as Captain pulls away. She looks sadly at Ethel, quiet and alone in the driveway. Turns and enters the house.

Not quite sure what to do now.

She goes into her room. The green notebook gleams menacingly from the place on the bed where she left it open.

Carefully Janie closes it and puts it in the box in the closet.

Drops to the bed and lies there, staring at the ceiling.

2:23 p.m.

The cool, damp wind blows briskly through Miss Stubin's dusky Center Street purgatory.

"Now you know as much as I know, Janie."

Janie sits silently next to Miss Stubin. Tears trickle from the old woman's blind eyes.

There are no more words to say. Only an understanding, a resolution, a small strength, passes and grows between them. And a release. Miss Stubin's work is done.

This is good-bye.

Slowly Miss Stubin squeezes Janie's hand with her own gnarled fingers. "I must go see my soldier now." And then she begins to fade away.

"Will I ever see you again?" Janie calls out anxiously.

"Not here, Janie."

"Somewhere else, then?" Her voice is hopeful.

But the old woman is already gone.

Janie looks around. Bites her lip. In front of the dry goods store strolls a young man in uniform and a bright-eyed young woman who turns to look over her shoulder. She blows a kiss at Janie as they turn the corner into the alley and disappear from sight.

Janie remains seated on the cold, wet park bench.

Alone.

March 31, 2006, 2:25 p.m.

Cabel dreams of layering clothes and more clothes on his body. Janie pulls herself out of it. She can't stand to watch him. She knows what the dream means. He's trying desperately to protect himself. His heart.

When the bell rings, Cabel startles awake. Janie watches him. He glances at her, looking worried. She pleads with him with her eyes across the vast library.

He drops his.

Turns.

Goes.

April 6, 2006, 8:53 a.m.

It's spring break. Janie awakes to a late spring snowfall, five fresh inches on the ground. Vows, one of these years, to go to Florida for spring break. Even if it means falling into dreams on the plane the entire way there. Even if it means spending the whole week alone, watching other people having fun.

She gets dressed and waits for the car Captain is sending. Brushes off Ethel so that the "For Sale" sign shows from the window again. Shovels the sidewalk and begins on the driveway. The snow is heavy and wet with the late-morning sun shining on it.

When Carrie bursts from her house next door and sprints through the yard, Janie grins.

"Hey," she says.

"Janie Hannagan!" Carrie says. "How dare you sell Ethel! Poor girl. Stu's a wreck over it."

Janie has been ready for this question. "I can't afford the insurance and the gas anymore, Carrie. Tell Stu I'm really sorry."

Carrie grins impishly. Whips out a wad of cash from her coat pocket. "How much?" she asks. "I'm selling my piece of junk. Ethel told me she wants to stay in the 'hood."

Janie's eyes light up. "No way!"

"*So* way!" Carrie giggles. "How much?"

Janie hops up and down in the snow. "For you? Twelve hundred bucks. It's a bargain!"

Carrie whips out twelve one-hundred-dollar bills and shoves them at Janie. "Sold!"

"Oh my gosh. I can't believe you're really buying Ethel!"

"Stu lent me the moolah until my car sells. He's probably happier than anyone. Now, take that sign out of the poor girl's window before she gets a complex! I gotta go call Stu and tell him we've got a deal. We'll figure out the paperwork later, cool?" Carrie lopes back to her house without waiting for an answer, while Janie, grinning, removes the sign from Ethel's window and lovingly pats the snowy hood.

It's Detective Jason Baker who picks her up, in his soccer-mom van. "Hey, little dreamer," he says with a grin. "I saw what you did to those bastards out on Durbin's deck. Remind me not to get in your way."

"I wish I remembered it," Janie says. She likes both Baker and Cobb.

"Still no memory of any of it, huh? Yeah, that's the way it is with those date-rape drugs. That's also why so many rapes go unnoticed or unreported. The memory loss allows sickos, like Durbin and his ilk, to get away with that shit time after time. You really saved the day, Janie."

Janie blushes and looks at her hands. She doesn't feel like much of a hero.

Inside the police station, Janie knocks on Captain's door.

"Come!" Captain yells, as usual.

Janie grins and enters.

Stops short.

Cabel is there too.

His smile is formal and strained as Janie gathers her composure and sits down next to him.

Captain gets down to business immediately.

"Stacey O'Grady will be returning to Fieldridge High, after all. Her parents are now satisfied that all the perps have been arrested, and Stacey really wants to put everything behind her and come back to graduate with her classmates."

Both Janie and Cabel nod. Janie's glad to hear it.

"There are several lawsuits in the works from various angry parents—and I don't blame them. But I'm afraid we're likely going to need you to testify, Janie. The hearings are set for June. You'll meet beforehand with the DA to go over your testimony. It could be difficult. So be prepared for some horrible questions to be asked of you by the defense attorneys. And you'll have to do it while Durbin, Wang, and Crater are sitting there, staring you down. You understand?"

Janie presses her lips together to stop them from quivering. "Yes, sir."

"Atta girl. We'll do everything within the law to keep your dream-catching ability a secret. However, it'll likely come out that you were at that party on assignment and working undercover for me. We'll need your story and your drug-tester sheets as evidence. If the perps are too stupid to plead guilty once they see the pile of evidence we have, we'll go to trial and your cover for Fieldridge assignments will probably be blown. But you need to tell the truth if asked, and we'll deal with it."

Janie's eyes widen. "So, um, if my cover is blown . . . will I . . . will you . . ."

Captain smiles. "You'll still have a job. No worries. Martha had a few close calls too, but her secret was never revealed on the stand. Defense attorneys don't know about dream catchers—They never think to ask the right questions. So, let's not fret about that right now, okay? I want you to take a little time off to relax and rejuvenate until school's out." Captain swivels in her chair and continues seamlessly, "And, Cabe, I've got some minor assignments for you starting Monday after school. Alone. Is that clear?" She looks at both of them.

"Yes, sir," Janie and Cabel say in unison.

"Will you two be able to work together again in the

future, or do I have to reconfigure my plans?" Captain asks bluntly.

Janie looks at Cabel. Cabel looks at his shoes.

"Yes, sir," Janie says finally. Daring Cabel to answer.

"Of course," Cabel says. He doesn't look at Janie.

Captain nods and shuffles the papers on her desk. "Good. Janie, see if Cobb or Baker or Rabinowitz is out there to give you a lift home. I'll talk with you soon."

"Yes, sir." Janie stands up, her face burning. Feeling like a baby in front of Cabe. She flees out the door, leaving Cabel and Captain standing there, and decides to walk home rather than beg for a ride.

She doesn't get far before Cabel's car whizzes past her, snow flying in his wake.

He slows.

Stops.

Backs up.

Janie glances longingly at the bushes, wishing for a place to hide.

Cabel lowers the passenger window and peers out at Janie. Smiles grimly. Bites his lip. "How about a ride, Hannagan?"

Janie nods coolly and gets in. Knows they're going to have to talk sometime if they're going to keep working together. "I can walk from your house so it's not too much trouble for you," she says civilly.

They ride in silence the entire way.

Cabel pulls into his driveway.

They get out.

Stare at each other for a minute, until Janie looks away, emotions welling up. She's angry. Still doesn't understand why he broke up with her so suddenly. Feels like it was because the teachers touched her. Wants to know the truth. But doesn't want to get shot down again. "Thanks for the ride," she finally says.

When he doesn't speak, doesn't move, she turns slowly and starts walking home.

GLIMMERS

"Wait," Cabel says.

Janie's been waiting. Waiting for answers. Waiting for him to admit that he can't touch her because she'd been violated by the creeps. Janie doesn't want to wait anymore. She walks faster.

He hesitates, and then runs after her. Stops her in the middle of the road. "Come inside with me," Cabel says. He looks tired. "Please. We need to talk."

Janie's eyes flash, but she follows him inside. Maybe at least she'll get some answers.

Janie sits on the edge of the living-room chair, leaving her coat on. She takes a deep breath and decides to get it over with. "You have three minutes to tell me that it's not because those bastards touched me."

Cabel reels. "What?"

Janie looks at her watch.

Cabel begins to pace.

"I can put up with the pacing," Janie says after a minute goes by. "I can put up with you having some issues you need to work out. I can even put up with you saying you just don't love me. I mean, I thought this weird dream curse would probably keep me from ever having a relationship, so I guess I'm lucky it lasted as long as it did. But when you suddenly decide you can't touch me anymore immediately after a bunch of jerks try to rape me, well, I just need to know if you are really that horrible. And if you are, it'll be a hell of a lot easier for me to walk out of here in"—she checks her watch—"one minute and twenty-four seconds."

He stares. His face is fraught with emotion. He walks over to Janie, kneels in front of her. His hands quiver as he touches her face.

She watches him solemnly. Gives him a chance.

"Janie," he finally says. "Is this the way it's going to be with you?"

Her eyes flash angrily as she squints at her watch.

"What? Stop changing the subject. You have one minute to say it's not because they touched me. Is it? Is that really it, Cabe? They touched me, and now I'm violated, and you can't stand to think of being with me again?"

"Oh god. You're serious?"

Janie's voice pitches higher. "Thirty seconds."

"Would you even believe me if I said it?" He's breathing hard. Stands abruptly and turns his back to her. His fingers rake through his hair.

"Fifteen seconds." Janie's voice is even, now. She stands up to leave.

He whirls around and grabs her arm. Pulls her to him. Kisses her hard, tangling his fingers in her hair. His tongue darts into her mouth and finds hers, tasting her, an oasis in the desert, his body urgently pressing against hers as his hands caress her neck.

Janie stands frozen for a moment, and then she moans and reaches for him. Cabel slips her coat off her shoulders, and it falls to the floor, and he lifts her up, holds her until she wraps her legs around his waist. His lips move to her neck and strain at the buttons of her shirt.

"Time's up," she says, gasping.

He lifts his lips from her skin. Runs his hand over her body. A button falls to the floor, bounces, and rolls under the chair. He walks, with her still attached, to the couch and sits with her on his lap. "Janie. Oh god, I can't do it," he whispers, and holds her tightly. Squeezes her. Just like she loves. "Janie," he says again. "I'm so messed up. Such an idiot. I'm sorry. No. I mean, the answer is no, it's not because they touched you. I just didn't know if I could handle this. You're too . . . I don't know. You're dangerous! I couldn't handle it. Couldn't handle loving you."

"What the heck does that mean? You didn't seem to have a problem being in love before. What happened?"

He gives her a miserable look. "What if I love you, give you everything I have inside me, open my heart up, and something horrible happens? What if you *did* get raped? It would change you so much, Janie. Change you forever. What if you get sucked into a dream while you're driving again? Have you thought through the consequences? To you? To others? To me, for god's sake. Janie, my father—He lit me. On. Fire. In that instant everything changed. I became a different person. Crap like that changes you. It scarred me, fucked up my life," he says. "In a bunch of ways." Cabel fingers the scars through his shirt as he talks. "I haven't let anybody inside since then, except for you. It's hard, Janie. It feels impossible. And then you go off being all reckless and shit. . . ." He takes a breath. "I needed safe, but I fell in love with you. Now I'm having a really shitty time dealing with the thought that something could happen to you. That you could change too. And I'd lose you."

Janie, jaw dropped, blinks. "You have a really funny way of showing it."

"I know. I . . . I'm fucked up. I thought it would be easier this way, you know? To take a break. It's just . . . It isn't . . ." He struggles for words. "This is intense, Janie. It scares the hell out of me. I wanted you to be my safe thing. No serious risks; just some simple dream stuff for Captain. Nothing like what you went through with Durbin! I mean, who the hell thought *that* would be your next assignment? God, wonder what comes next . . ."

"So you broke up with me because you couldn't handle it if I changed or got hurt or left you. Is that what you're saying? Doesn't everyone have to take that risk? Do you still love me or don't you?" Janie's lip quivers. She thinks about all the changes that will be happening to her in the next years, and feels Cabel slipping away again.

"I'm saying I love you and I'm still learning. . . . I want to learn how to deal with that. All I know is that I thought this break would help, but all it's doing is making me batshit crazy." Cabel pauses. Smiles weakly. "So, um, can you please just not do anything dangerous? Isn't life bad enough when you can't control what the nightmares do to you? Do you really have to take even more risks?"

Janie smiles ruefully. She wraps her arms around his neck and rests her head on his shoulder. Thinking. "What if I do get hurt? Or if something . . . happens to me. Will you stop loving me?" she asks quietly.

"How could I?" Cabel strokes her hair. "But I have to learn how to handle the feelings that come with that. I'm just not used to caring about something, about someone, so much that it hurts. Not like this."

Janie is quiet, thoughtful. "Did you know that you were the first person I ever remember saying 'I love you' to? I don't even remember saying it to my mother. Which is really sad."

"I didn't know," he says. He lets his head fall back on the couch and takes a deep breath. Lets it out. "Do you still love me, Janie?"

Janie stares at him, incredulous. "Yes, of course! I don't say it lightly."

"Say it lightly in my ear," he demands.

She smiles, rests her soft cheek on his scratchy one, and whispers it. "I love you, Cabe."

They sit, holding each other. And then Cabel asks her, "Truth or dare?"

Janie blinks. "Do I really have an option here?"

"No," Cabel says. "Okay, um . . ." Takes a deep breath. "What's happening to you, Janie? I just . . . I need to know. Please." He shifts her, so he can see her eyes.

They fill with tears.

He straightens her glasses and takes a deep breath. "Tell me," he says.

Janie bites her lip. "Nothing, Cabe. I'm fine." She can't look at him.

Cabel rips his fingers through his hair. "Just . . . just say it. Get it out there, so we can deal with it. You're going blind from all the dreams, aren't you."

Janie blinks. Her lips part in surprise.

He touches her cheek, stroking it with his thumb.

"What . . . how . . . ?" she begins.

"You squint, even with your glasses on. You get headaches all the time. Bright light bothers you. It takes you longer to get your sight back after each dream you get sucked into." He pauses. Anxious. "And then, in the hospital, when you weren't sucked into anyone's dream, but you were having your own nightmare, you couldn't see when you woke up. That was the first time for that, wasn't it?"

She sinks back into his shoulder. Doesn't remember that dream in the hospital. Also doesn't want to cry anymore. "Damn," she says. "You're a good detective."

"How soon?" he whispers.

She presses her lips to his cheek, and then she sighs. "A few years."

He takes in a sharp breath and slowly lets it out again. "Okay. What else, Janie."

She closes her eyes, resigned. "My hands," she says. "They'll be gnarled and ugly and useless in fifteen years."

He waits, stroking her back. "Anything else?" His voice is anxious.

"Not really," she whispers. "Just . . . I can't drive anymore. Ever again." She loses her fight with the tears. "Poor Ethel. At least she's got a good home now."

He holds her, rocking, stroking her hair. "Janie," he says after a while. "How old was Miss Stubin when she died?"

"In her seventies."

He breathes a sigh. "Oh. Thank god."

"Can you deal with this, Cabel? Because if you can't . . ." She chokes. "If you can't, tell me now."

He looks into her eyes.

Touches her cheek.

4:22 p.m.

Cabel calls Captain.

"Komisky."

"Sir, any chance Janie and I can be seen together now?"

"Under the circumstances, that would pretty damn much make my day, yes. Besides, the Wilder cocaine case got settled on Monday. He pleaded guilty."

"You rock, sir."

"Yes, yes, I know. Go out to a movie or something, will you?"

"Right away. Thank you."

"And stop bothering me."

"Good-bye, sir."

"Take care. Both of you."

Cabel smiles and hangs up. "Guess what."

"What," Janie says.

"We can go out on our first date."

"Woo hoo!"

"And guess what else—You're buying."

"Me? Why?"

"Because you lost the bet."

Janie thinks a moment. Punches Cabel in the arm. "You did not fail five quizzes or tests!"

"I did. I have proof."

"Shit!"

"Yep."

DON'T LOOK BACK

May 24, 2006, 7:06 p.m.

Janie strides into the Fieldridge High School auditorium, where hundreds of parents, grandparents, brothers, and sisters are seated in bleachers, folding chairs, and balcony seats, and waving programs near their soppy necks in ninety-five-degree heat and humidity. It seems the old building's air-conditioning can't take the pressure of another graduation ceremony.

She glances around and spots Cabel several rows behind her. He blows an impish kiss, and she grins. Her cap's band threatens to squeeze her brain into mush, and she feels the sweat soaking into it.

Janie looks in the other direction, scanning the

audience. Some familiar faces. Carrie's parents sit off to the side on the wooden bleachers, and Janie offers a small smile, even though they aren't looking at her.

Even with her newly updated prescription glasses, it's difficult to see far away. Colors bleed from one dress to the next. But finally Janie spots her. It's the bronze hair contrasted with her dark skin that helps. Sitting next to Captain is a large man who looks like Denzel Washington, twenty years from now. His arm is spread lazily across the back of Captain's chair. Janie can see Captain poke her husband and point. Janie squints and smiles, and then lowers her eyes. She's not sure why.

The valedictorian takes the stage, and the crowd quiets, leaving only the rush of flapping programs.

It's not Cabel.

Thankfully.

He managed to pull his grades down successfully to a mere 3.93. Third place. Enough to keep him out of the limelight. Which is all he wants, really. Janie's not far behind with a 3.85. She's thrilled.

There are three faculty chairs empty in the auditorium this year. Doc, Happy, and Dumbass. Suspended without pay. Awaiting the hearing. Janie feels a pang of sadness for those chairs.

Not for the men who sat there.

Just so we're clear.

Even so.

They are reminders of pain and embarrassment, horror wrapped up like a gift. Janie's glad that box exploded.

Up at the microphone, Stacey O'Grady begins speaking. She has a different air about her now. New, in the past few months. Reserved. Solemn. A maturity, perhaps, or a sense of understanding that not all things turn out the way you'd wish them to.

Janie's mother isn't there.

Neither is Cabel's, but no one expected her. Although Cabel's older brother, Charlie, and Charlie's wife, Megan, are somewhere in the crowd.

Expectations. It's what they always talk about at these things. Making a difference in the future. Striving for excellence. Blah, blah, blah.

Janie wipes a drop of sweat from her forehead. Looks around as Stacey says from the podium, "The best years are yet to come," and Janie watches the room explode in applause.

Janie doesn't join them.

The ominous words ring in her ears.

The crowd of seniors stands and, one by one, over the course of an hour, their names are called. Janie steps carefully across the stage, prays that the little sleeping baby nearby doesn't dream yet, and takes her diploma. Shakes hands with Abernethy. Moves her tassel over to the other side. Walks lightly down the stage stairs and back to her folding chair to wait.

When the stage is silent and Principal Abernethy gives one last word of congratulations, the hats fly and the voices around Janie rise to fill the auditorium. Janie takes her hat off her head and tucks it under her arm, waiting, waiting. Waiting to be done. So she can say good-bye to this place, once and for all.

When the madhouse clears, she's still standing there. Only a few lingerers remain in the building that now feels like a rain forest after a downpour. She walks slowly down the aisle toward the exit steps, where she'll meet Cabel and whoever else he's schmoozing with. But for now, she is alone.

The custodian comes by with a broom, and he smiles at her. Janie nods and smiles in return, and he begins sweeping the wood-floored aisles that most often serve as a basketball court. And then the lights fade a bit.

Janie blinks and leans against the wall, just in case.

But it's no one's dream.

It's just the end of some things.

And the beginning of others.

Lisa McMann is the *New York Times* bestselling author of *Wake*, *Fade*, and *Gone*. She grew up in Michigan and now lives in the Phoenix area with her husband and two kids. Read more about Lisa at LisaMcMann.com or find her on Facebook, Myspace, or Twitter.

Praise for *Fade*

"A great blend of mystery, romance, and supernatural elements, and featuring a strong but vulnerable female protagonist, this episode ends with an irresistible hook for the final instalment." —*Booklist*

"The quick-paced, present-tense narration and realistic dialogue that gripped readers in the first book resume here . . . Fans will clamor for a third title." —*Kirkus Reviews*

"Gripping, imaginative . . . Fans of the first book will not be disappointed." —*Grand Rapids Press*

"As a highly anticipated sequel to *Wake*, *Fade* certainly lives up to expectations." —TeensReadToo.com

"Intriguing . . . the spare but effective narrative holds readers' attention." —*SLJ*

A *New York Times* Bestseller

Read a sneak preview
of the thrilling final instalment
in the Wake Trilogy

Gone

by Lisa McMann

Static and shockingly bright colors. Again, Janie nearly crumples to her knees, but this time she is more prepared. She steps blindly toward the bed and Cabel helps her safely to the floor as her head pounds with noise. It's more intense than ever.

Just when Janie thinks her eardrums are going to burst, the static dulls and the scene flickers to a woman in the dark once again. It's the same woman as the day before, Janie's certain, though she can't make out any distinguishing features. And then Janie sees that the man is there too. It's Henry, of course. It's his dream. He's in the shadows, sitting on a chair, watching the woman. Henry turns, looks at Janie and blinks. His eyes widen and he sits up straighter in his chair. "Help me!" he pleads.

And then, like a broken filmstrip, the picture cuts out and the static is back, louder than ever, constant screamo in her ears. Janie struggles, head pounding. Tries pulling out of the dream, but she can't focus—the static is messing up her ability to concentrate.

She's flopping around on the floor now. Straining.

Thinks Cabel is there, holding her, but she can't feel anything now.

The bright colors slam into her eyes, into her brain, into her body. The static is like pinpricks in every pore of her skin.

She's trapped.

Trapped in the nightmare of a man who can't wake up.

Janie struggles again, feeling like she's suffocating now. Feeling like if she doesn't get out of this mess, she might die here. Cabe! she screams in her head. Get me out of here!

But of course he can't hear her.

She gathers up all her strength and pulls, groaning inwardly with such force that it hurts all the way through. When the nightmare flickers to the picture of the woman again, Janie is just borely able to burst from her confines.

She gasps for breath.

"Janie?" Cabel's voice is soft, urgent.

His finger paints her skin from forehead to cheek, his hand captures the back of her neck, and then he lifts her, carries her to the chair. "Are you okay?"

Janie can't speak. She can't see. Her body is numb. All she can do is nod.

And then, there's a sound from across the room.

It's certainly not Henry.

Janie hears Cabel swear under his breath.

"Good morning," says a man. "I'm Doctor Ming."

Janie sits up as straight as she can in the cha1r, hoping Cabel's standing in front of her.

"Hi," Cabe says. "We—I—how's he doing today? We just got here."

Dr. Ming doesn't answer immediately and Janie breaks out into a sweat. *Oh, God, he's staring at me.*

"Are you . . . ?"

"We're his kids."

"And is the young woman all right?"

"She's fine. This is really . . ." Cabel sighs and his voice catches. "Ah . . . really an emotional time for us, you know." Janie knows he's stalling for her sake.

"Of course," says the doctor. "Well."

Janie's sight is beginning to return and she sees that Dr. Ming is glancing over the chart. He continues. "It could be any day or he might hang on for a few. It's hard to say."

Janie clears her throat and leans carefully to the side of the chair so she can see past Cabel's bum. "Is he . . . brain-dead?"

"Hm? No, there appears to be some minor brain activity still."

"What's wrong with him, exactly?"

"We don't actually know. Could be a tumor, maybe a series of strokes. And without surgery, we might not ever know. But he made it clear in his DNR that he didn't want life-saving measures and his next of kin—your mother, I believe?—she refused to sign off on surgery or any procedures." He says this in a pitying voice that makes Janie hate him.

"Well," she says, "does he even have insurance?"

The doctor checks the paperwork again. "Apparently not."

"What are the chances that surgery will help? I mean, could he be normal again?"

Dr. Ming glances at Henry, as if he can determine his chances by looking at him. "I don't know. He might never be able to live on his own. That is, if he even survived the surgery." He looks at the chart again.

Janie nods slowly. That's why. That's why he's just lying here. That, and the DNR. That's why they aren't fixing him—he's too broken. She tries to sound simply curious but it comes out nervous. "So, uh, how much does it cost for him to just be here, waiting to die . . . and stuff?"

The doctor shakes his head. "I don't know—that's really a question for the accounting office." He glances at his watch. Puts the chart back. "Okay, then." He walks briskly out of the room, pulling the door closed behind him.

When Dr. Ming is gone, Janie glares at Cabel. "Don't ever let that happen again! Couldn't you tell I was trapped in the nightmare? I couldn't get out, Cabe. I thought I was going to die."

Cabel's mouth opens, surprised and hurt. "I could tell you were struggling, but if I did break it, how was I supposed to know you wouldn't be mad at me for that? And what did you want me to do, drag you out in the hallway? We're in a freaking hospital, Hannagan. If anybody saw you like that you'd be strapped to a gurney in thirty seconds and we'd be stuck here all day, not to mention the bill for that."

"Better that than sucked into full frontal static-land. No wonder the guy's crazy. I'm half-crazy just spending a few minutes listening to that. Besides," Janie adds coolly, pointing to the private bathroom, "hello."

Cabel rolls his eyes. "I didn't think of it, okay? You know, it's not like I spend every waking moment planning my life around your stupid problems. There's more—"

He slams his lips together.

Janie's jaw drops.

"Oh, crap." He steps toward her, sorry-eyed. And she steps back.

Shakes her head and looks away, fingers to her mouth, eyes filling.

"Don't, Janie. I didn't mean it."

Janie closes her eyes and swallows hard. "No," she says slowly. Doesn't want to say it, but knows it's true. "You're right. I'm sorry." She gives a morose laugh. "It's good for you to say it like it is, you know? Healthy. And shit."

"Come on," he says. "Come 'ere." He steps toward her again and this time she goes to him. He runs his fingers through her hair and holds her to his chest. Kisses her forehead. "I'm sorry too. And that's not like it is. I just . . . it just came out wrong."

"Did it? Are you really saying that you aren't concerned about what's going to happen to me? About how that will affect you?"

"Janie—" Cabel gives her a helpless look.

"Well?"

"Well what? What do you want me to say?"

"I want you to tell the truth. Aren't you worried? Not even a little bit?"

"Janie," he says again. "Don't. Why are you doing this?"

But he doesn't answer the question.

To Janie, that says it all. She closes her eyes. "I think I'm a little stressed out," she whispers after a moment, and then shakes her head. At least now she knows. "Got a lot on my mind."

"Oh, really?" Cabe laughs softly.

'Some great vacation week, huh?"

Cabel snorts. "Yeah. Seems like forever since we were lazing around in the sun."

Janie's quiet, thinking about her mother, her father, and everything else. Cabel, and her own stupid problems, as Cabel calls them. And now, she wonders, *Who's going to pay this hospital bill?* She hopes like hell Henry has money, but by the looks of him, he's homeless. "No insurance," she groans aloud. Bangs her head against Cabel's chest. "Ay yi yi."

"It's not your problem."

Janie sighs deeply. "Why do I feel so responsible for it then?"

Cabel's quiet.

Janie looks up at him. "What?"

"You want me to analyze you?"

She laughs. "Sure."

"I'll probably regret saying anything. But it's like this. You're so used to playing the responsible one with your mother. Now you see this dysfunctional guy, somebody tells you he's your father and boom, your instinct is to be responsible for him, too, since he appears to be even more fucked-up than your mother. God knows we never thought that was possible."

Janie sighs. "I'm just trying to get through it all, you know? Get through the messes one by one, hoping each time it's the last one, and then I look beyond it and realize, crap, there's one more. Just hoping that someday, finally, I'll be free." Janie looks over at Henry and walks over to the side of the bed. "But it never happens," she says. Looks at her father for a long moment.

Thinking.

Thinking.

Maybe it's time to change.

Time to be responsible for just one person.

I